# Don't Think About
# TOMORROW

ANNE SCHRAFF

SADDLEBACK
EDUCATIONAL PUBLISHING

# URBAN UNDERGROUND ®

**SADDLEBACK**
EDUCATIONAL PUBLISHING
www.sdlback.com

ISBN-13: 978-1-61651-664-2
ISBN-10: 1-61651-664-X
eBook: 978-1-61247-358-1

Printed in Guangzhou, China
1011/CA21101701

17 16 15 14 13   1 2 3 4 5

# CHAPTER ONE

Lydell Nelson had been going to Harriet Tubman High School for three years. He was a senior now, but hardly anyone in the class knew him. He was slightly overweight, wore glasses, and always chose to eat alone. During lunch he was always writing in a journal. Nobody ever bothered to ask him what he was writing, and he never volunteered any information. Many students attended Tubman High. Many strong friendships had been forged when the kids were freshmen or even before then, at Marian Anderson Middle School. Little groups of students always ate lunch and hung out together. Lydell didn't belong to any of these groups. He seemed to be a lonely person. But, when people tried to be friends, he turned them away.

Some people thought he was crazy. Some even thought he was dangerous.

Sami Archer, a senior, was also a little overweight. She was always on the lookout for the lonely outsider. She had noticed Lydell way back in tenth grade when he first appeared at Tubman. Sami had a radiant smile and a bubbly personality. If anybody could bring someone into her circle of friends, Sami could. But Lydell politely turned aside all her efforts and went his way. Sami didn't know why.

"He's weird," Sami confided in her closest friend, Alonee Lennox. Alonee was very lovely and popular. "He all the time writing away in that journal. I wonder what he's writing there. It's almost like he's a time traveler or something. Like he's taking notes about us."

"Maybe he's writing a novel," Alonee suggested. "The great American novel."

One of the senior English teachers was Langston Myers. He was actually a writer with poems published in obscure literary journals like *Mississippi Mud Ink*. He was paid for his work in copies of the journals. Some of the more unkind students, like Marko Lane, enjoyed making fun of him. Marko found Mr. Myers's poems in *Bayou Bard* on the Internet. He read them aloud to amuse his friends. Jasmine Benson, Marko's girlfriend, howled in laughter. Then word got around that Myers had written a novel and that he was having trouble getting it published. Marko found more humor in that.

But nobody was sure what Lydell Nelson was up to.

"He's probably terribly lonely," Sereeta Prince told her boyfriend, Jaris Spain. "I feel sorry for him. He sort of hides in that journal."

Sereeta and her friends always went to lunch together. They ate in a special spot at Tubman under some eucalyptus trees.

Alonee Lennox had originally gathered all of them together, and they were called Alonee's "posse." The group included Kevin Walker and his girlfriend, Carissa Polson. Derrick Shaw, Destini Fletcher, and Alonee's boyfriend, Oliver Randall, were also in the group. Sami Archer was often the center of things.

When they were at their lunch spot, Jaris made an announcement. "Pop did something he's never done before. He's been cooking a lot lately, but he never packed lunches for me and Chelsea. My little sister, chili pepper, she was watching Pop make our lunches. She said it's Swiss cheese, corned beef, creamy coleslaw on rye bread. I'm tellin' you guys, I'm ready for lunch!"

"Trade you a dried-up chicken breast on white bread," Alonee giggled.

"No way," Jaris laughed. He'd been thinking about Pop's sandwich all morning.

Munching on his sandwich, Jaris looked over at Lydell. He was sitting by himself. "I've smiled at Lydell," Jaris remarked, "and said 'hi.' But he sorta ignores me. I even asked him to join us for lunch a couple times. But he didn't want to."

"I've asked him to come with us to lunch too," Sereeta said. "I smiled at him and he didn't even smile back."

"Anybody who wouldn't smile back at you, girl, has got to be one sick puppy," Sami Archer laughed.

"You can't force people to be friendly," Kevin Walker asserted. "I remember when I first came here from Texas. Alonee, you were chattering away and trying to make me feel at home. But I wasn't ready for it. But eventually you guys won me over."

Kevin finished his lunch and stretched out on the grass, looking at the clouds building in the sky. The weatherman promised rain, and Kevin was hoping for it. Back in Texas the clouds would gather quickly, and drenching rain would fall. It made everything green, and the creeks ran fast. Kevin was kind of a loner himself. He knew where Lydell was coming from. Kevin carried a dark secret when he came to Tubman as a junior. His father had murdered a man, and he died in prison. That cast a shadow over Kevin's life. He thought maybe Lydell had dark secrets too.

"Maybe he just doesn't need anybody," Sami mused thoughtfully. "I guess there's people like that. I don't understand 'em, but they out there. Makes you wonder, though. He okay, or he got bad feelings swirling in his soul? Maybe we think he's just happy bein' a loner, so we give him his space. But maybe he's thinkin' we all hate him and he's fixin' to explode."

From their comfortable place under the eucalyptus trees, they could see Lydell sitting on one of the stone benches on campus. He always brought his lunch in a brown bag. It was always a sandwich and cottage cheese. He'd quickly finish his lunch and then start writing again in his journal.

Oliver Randall also joined Alonee's posse at Tubman after he moved from Los

Angeles. His father taught astronomy at the community college, and his mother sang opera. Oliver was bursting with personality and good looks. He wanted as many friends as he could get. Oliver asked, "Has anybody ever just walked up to Lydell and asked him what he was writing in his journal? Maybe he'd open up."

"Don't look at me," Jaris Spain protested. He was a warm, friendly guy, but he wasn't pushy. "To tell the truth, the guy sort of freaks me out. I've said stuff to him. Like there's a test coming up and is he ready, 'cause I'm not. And he didn't even answer me. At first I thought maybe he didn't speak English. I thought he was from some country in Africa where they spoke French or something. But then I heard him answer in class. He speaks regular English, no accent."

"I'm really curious," Oliver asserted with a grin. "I think I'll just do what my dad always says. I'll grab the bull by the horns. I'll walk up there and ask him what he's writing in his journal."

Trevor Jenkins was another member of Alonee's posse and Jaris's best friend. Trevor shook his head. "I wouldn't bother that dude, Oliver. I'm with Jaris. He freaks me."

The others knew Lydell from years back, even though they were not friends with him. But being new himself at Tubman, Oliver hadn't seen Lydell for very long. Oliver walked up the little path leading from the stand of eucalyptus trees. He slowly approached Lydell Nelson. The boy had finished his lunch and was writing in his journal. He had a spiral notebook and a ballpoint pen.

"Hi," Oliver greeted. "I'm Oliver Randall. I came to Tubman in my junior year."

Lydell ignored Oliver and continued writing in his spiral notebook.

"Uh, you're Lydell Nelson, right?" Oliver asked.

"Yes," Lydell replied. "What is it that you want?"

"Uh, nothing," Oliver said. "I just see you writing in your journal all the time. I was curious. I wondered if you were writing a novel or something. That's interesting to me 'cause I try to write short stories sometimes."

Lydell looked at Oliver for another moment. Then he returned to his writing. He didn't say anything else. Oliver walked back down to the eucalyptus trees, where his friends were waiting. They had seen what happened. Both Jaris and Trevor had half smiles on their faces that said, "I told you so, dude."

Oliver shook his head. "He's got the coldest look in his eyes. I've never seen such a cold look," he commented.

Jaris nodded and agreed. "That's why he freaks me out. I can make friends with most people but . . ."

Kevin was still lying on the grass. He was still watching the clouds form into odd shapes. His mother, who died last year, used to go for walks with Kevin. She'd point out the shapes of animals and people in the clouds. It was fun walking with her in

Texas and picking out animal shapes in the sky. Now Kevin remarked, "Maybe Lydell has demons. Just leave him be. Some guys have demons."

Kevin himself had had demons. He was such a fast runner back home in Texas that his mother nicknamed him "Twister." He reminded her of a tornado. But Kevin struggled with a bad temper. Last year, when Marko Lane bullied Kevin, he almost killed the bully. Kevin was about to beat Marko up when he heard his dead mother's voice pleading, "No, Twister, no!"

"It's scary to think what dark corners we have in our minds," Sereeta commented.

"Yeah," Kevin agreed.

After lunch, Sereeta and Jaris walked to Mr. Myers' English class. Lydell Nelson sat in the last row. Sereeta always noticed that Lydell seemed very intent on Mr. Myers' lecture. Maybe, she thought, Lydell *was* writing a novel in that journal. Maybe because Mr. Myers was a novelist too, they had something in common.

As Sereeta and Jaris walked toward English, Jaris put his arm around her shoulders. She seemed so small and delicate. He wanted to protect her. He'd wanted to do that since middle school. She was always a lovely, fragile beauty. Her parents had divorced and left her on her own. She often cried over the chaos in her life.

Sereeta's parents each remarried after the divorce. She had been living with her mom and stepfather, Perry Manley. But she never liked her stepfather. And Mom was in rehab, recovering from an alcohol and depression problem. So now Sereeta was staying with her grandmother.

Sereeta was trying to get along better with her stepfather. She was worried about how it would be when her mother got home next month. Sereeta sure wouldn't be helping her mom if she and her stepfather weren't getting along.

"You and your stepdad doing a little better since you talked the other day?" Jaris asked.

"Yeah," Sereeta replied. "He asked me out to a restaurant tonight. He wants to talk some more. I'm kinda nervous about it. I'm not looking forward to sitting there through a whole meal trying to say the right thing."

"I guess this is maybe a crazy idea, Sereeta," Jaris suggested. "But would it help if someone was there with you?"

Sereeta turned and looked at Jaris, her eyes filling with hope. "Oh Jaris, that would be so fabulous!" she responded. "Would you really come? Would you do that for me?"

"Babe, for you I'd do anything," Jaris smiled at her. "Of course I'd come, but do you think that'd be okay with your step-father?"

"Yeah, I think he'd be more comfortable too if it wasn't just the two of us," Sereeta replied. "We've, you know, been sort of enemies for so long. There's so much garbage. Jaris, you have this great personality that it'd just make everything better."

"I don't know about that, babe," Jaris protested, "but I'll do my best."

"Oh wow!" Sereeta exclaimed. "Now I don't feel nearly as bad about tonight."

"So, I'll pick you up at your grandma's. We'll drive to the restaurant and meet your stepdad there," Jaris asked. "Then I'll take you home."

"We're eating at Angelo's," Sereeta said. "It's a reasonably priced place just off Algonquin. You sure it won't be too much trouble, Jaris?"

"Sereeta," Jaris sighed, "don't you get it yet? I would do anything in the world for you."

"Jaris . . ." she cooed.

"I love you, babe," Jaris told her. "I'd walk through Death Valley in August for you."

Sereeta leaned in close to him as they went down the pathway to English. She smiled up at him and wondered, "What did I ever do to deserve you?"

"Likewise," Jaris agreed.

The couple took a few more steps together in silence. "Your mom," Jaris remarked, "is gonna be so relieved when she gets home. You know, if you and your stepfather are getting along better. I think that's gonna do her a lot of good."

As Jaris and Sereeta neared the classroom door, Mr. Myers hadn't arrived yet. Lydell was coming from another direction. He passed them, hurried into the classroom, and took his usual seat in the back. The boy opened his spiral notebook and began writing. Suddenly, Jaris heard a familiar but unwelcome voice.

"Hey Lydell," Marko Lane taunted as he walked in, "you still writing in that book? You a spy from Transylvania or somethin'? Takin' notes on us to give to Dracula?"

Marko had found a new target for his bullying, Lydell.

Lydell continued writing, ignoring Marko.

"Look at that dude, Jasmine," Marko remarked to his girlfriend, Jasmine Benson. "He don't stop writing for a minute. Hey man, level with us. What's up with you? You're making us all nervous. Like, you gonna put stuff about us on YouTube or something?"

"Knock it off, Lane," Kevin growled. "Mind your own business."

"Uh . . . I'm just trying to be friendly to poor old Lydell here," Marko protested with mock innocence. "He's got a big problem. He's a weird loner. We need to help this dude find a place in the real world."

Mr. Myers came in then, slamming his expensive briefcase down on the desk. Last year for junior English, they had Mr. Pippin. His briefcase looked as if it was falling apart. Unlike Mr. Pippin, Mr. Myers was not frightened of his students. Mr. Pippin would look out over the class like a cowed animal. He was always waiting for the next outrage from Marko Lane and his friends.

But Mr. Myers was angry and arrogant. He glared at the students. He acted as if they were all way below his intelligence level. He seemed as though it was tragic that he had to waste his time with them. He respected only one of his students: Oliver Randall, who was kind of a genius. Mr. Myers saw himself as a brilliant novelist on the verge of being discovered by the critics. Getting his book published would free him forever of having to deal with high school students. What fueled Mr. Myers's anger was that stupid editors kept sending his book manuscript back, rejected. Each rejection only delayed his liberation from teaching senior English.

"It is an abomination," Jaris heard Mr. Myers declaring to Mr. Pippin the other day. "You send out a great manuscript, and some book companies don't even have the courtesy to return it. Instead they shred it, even when you have included a self-addressed stamped envelope. The Neanderthals now in charge of publishing are unfit to edit alphabet books."

"Terrible, terrible!" Mr. Pippin agreed, though he had never tried to sell anything he had written. He wrote a few letters to the local newspaper about pet peeves, but even these never saw print. Mr. Pippin was always so busy trying to keep discipline in his classroom that he had no time to write. He barely had time to write his checks at the end of the month. Mr. Pippin looked up to Mr. Myers. Mr. Myers was quite a bit younger. He seemed superior to Mr. Pippin in education and in his ability to control a classroom.

Now everyone grew quiet as Mr. Myers began to lecture. Even Marko Lane knew better than to create a disturbance. When the lecture began, Lydell Nelson looked up, his dark eyes behind his thick glasses seeming to grow even larger. Jaris had been in classes with Lydell before, and he often seemed disinterested. He seemed to view Mr. Pippin with contempt last year, though he earned good grades. This year, he seemed enthralled by Mr. Myers.

"I am going to recite a very famous quote from literature," Mr. Myers announced. "One that comments powerfully on the human condition. I want you to listen to the quote and to tell me the meaning it has for you. I also want you to identify the author if you can."

In his powerful baritone, Mr. Myers intoned the quotation: "'The mass of men lead lives of quiet desperation.'"

Marko Lane raised his hand. He wanted very much to get on the good side of Mr. Myers. At the beginning of the semester, Marko had stumbled badly. Marko had been snapping his fingers to a rap song in his mind. Mr. Myers went ballistic. Then, to make matters worse, Marko pretended to like one of Mr. Myers's poems in an obscure journal. Marko called it by the wrong title and obviously didn't understand it. That only annoyed Mr. Myers more. Now, in a grand effort to redeem himself, Marko stated, "Those are very fine words, Mr. Myers. I bet you wrote them. They sound like something you wrote."

In spite of the discipline in the class-room, uncontrollable laughter broke out. Even Oliver Randall was laughing. Mr. Myers looked as though he could have killed Marko on the spot. Then, as the laughter died, Lydell Nelson spoke up in a shrill, high-pitched voice. "Henry David Thoreau wrote that. It means we are mostly miserable. But we hide the fact from the world because nobody cares."

"That's right, Mr. Nelson," Mr. Myers said approvingly. "Can you expand on that?"

"Yeah," Lydell replied. "It means you keep on going and doing your own thing. You're frustrated, but you hide it."

Alonee raised her hand. "The quote is very sad," she commented. "It means that most people are unhappy, but they pretend they're okay. They believe people don't want to see your heartache."

"It's kind of a fatalistic attitude," Oliver Randall added. "If people feel that bad, maybe they can do something to change their lives."

"Sometimes you can't change things," Lydell countered in an animated voice. "Sometimes you're trapped. You can't get out of where you are. You're looking for an escape hatch but there isn't one." Jaris had never heard so much passion in a classroom discussion. "Lot of people like that. You see 'em in cars on the freeway. Like rats trapped in their cars. They're trapped by other people in their lives or by stuff they can't change. We're trapped right here at this school. A lot of us don't want to be here. We hate it, but we can't get out!"

A moment or so of silence followed Lydell's little speech. Even Mr. Myers was quiet. Jaris glanced back at Lydell. He seemed to be shaking with emotion. The boy was getting a little scary. Usually he was so absorbed in his writing that he seemed oblivious to everything. The Thoreau quote seemed to unlock deep feelings.

# CHAPTER TWO

After class, Jaris, Alonee, and Oliver stood talking. Marko Lane and Jasmine stood nearby. Marko glanced over at Jaris and asked, "Did you hear that guy—Lydell? Somethin' wrong there. He looks like he's got a screw loose or somethin'. That guy gives me the creeps, I'm tellin' you."

Jaris was worried whenever he agreed with Marko Lane about anything. Now he sort of did. There *was* something wrong with Lydell Nelson. He needed to talk to somebody, maybe a school counselor.

Jaris saw Lydell walking slowly out of the classroom. On the spur of the moment, Jaris followed him. "Hey Lydell," Jaris called out.

Lydell turned around and glared at Jaris. "What do you want?" he demanded.

"Take it easy, man," Jaris said. "You just seemed so upset. I wondered if you were all right. You doin' okay, dude?"

"Yes," Lydell asserted. "Are you?"

Lydell seemed so hostile that Oliver Randall joined in. "Henry David Thoreau really understood human nature," he offered. "Have you read many of his works, Lydell?"

Lydell said nothing for a moment. Then he recited in a belligerent voice, "*Walden, A Week on the Concord and Merrimack Rivers, The Maine Woods.*"

"Good for you," Oliver said.

Lydell turned and walked away.

Jaris watched Lydell disappear around a corner. "You think we should tell somebody?" Jaris asked Sereeta.

Sereeta shrugged. "Tell who what?" she asked.

Oliver and Alonee stood there too. Oliver remarked, "I'm not sure it's any of our business, Jaris. The guy is real uptight, but it's a free country, right? We have the constitutional right to be weird."

"Here, here," Kevin Walker affirmed.

"He's crazy!" Marko Lane declared. "I always thought he was crazy, writin' all the time."

"I'm scared of people like that," Jasmine said. "Sometimes they just go off."

"I suppose we could tell a school counselor or something," Alonee suggested. "But I don't want to make trouble for the guy."

"How about if we talk to Ms. McDowell?" Jaris suggested. Torie McDowell was now teaching Jaris, Oliver, Alonee, and Marko AP American History. She was probably the best and the most compassionate teacher at the school. She was not only a skilled and inspiring teacher, but she genuinely cared about her students. Jaris admired her very much. In fact, she was a big reason he was thinking about teaching as a career. "Ms. McDowell is great working with kids," he concluded.

"Yeah, I like that idea," Sereeta agreed. "When I was feeling really down, she helped me a lot. Let's go see her."

"She can't do anything," Marko objected. "Lydell's a nut case. A whack job."

Kevin Walker looked at Marko and sneered, "It takes one to know one, Lane."

After the last class, Jaris, Sereeta, Alonee, and Oliver went to Ms. McDowell's classroom. She always stayed a while after school, and she was available to her students. She was the most open and helpful teacher Jaris ever met.

Ms. McDowell was a beautiful woman in her early thirties. She had come from a rough background. Her family was wracked by drugs, and she had lost both parents at an early age. With almost miraculous grit and determination, she rose above that hardship. Now she was helping her younger brother, Shane Burgess, to overcome drugs and the lure of the streets. Ms. McDowell took him into her condo, and she was hoping he could soon return to Tubman High.

"Hi, Ms. McDowell," Jaris said. She had a special feeling for Jaris. He was not only smart, but very reliable. More than once he had come through for Ms. McDowell when she was handling a bad situation on the campus. "You got a couple minutes?"

"Sure," the teacher agreed with a smile.

"There's this student, a senior now," Jaris began. "He's been at Tubman for three years, and none of us really know him. He's a loner, and he's always writing in this journal. He never talks to anyone unless you force him to. Even then, he seems angry all the time. His name is Lydell Nelson, and we're sorta worried about him."

"He seems really angry and troubled by something," Sereeta added. "But when you reach out, he blows you off."

"I know Lydell," Ms. McDowell commented. "He was in one of my classes last year. He's a very good student."

"Maybe you could just sort of talk to him, like a counselor would," Oliver suggested. "Maybe he'd open up with you."

"Thanks for the heads-up, you guys," Ms. McDowell said. "We'll see what we can do." That was all she said. She was too professional to discuss anything more specific. But Jaris and the others felt something good would happen. And they felt good that they had *done something*. They didn't just blow it off.

"Thanks, Ms. McDowell," Jaris said, walking out with his friends.

Outside, Jaris sighed, "Man, I feel better!" The others agreed. They felt the same way. "Well," he went on, "gotta go pick up chili pepper."

Chili pepper was Chelsea, Jaris's four-teen-year-old sister. She was grounded by their parents. She had gotten into trouble while still at Marian Anderson Middle School. Now she was a freshman at Tub-man. Jaris had to deliver her and pick her up every day.

Chelsea jumped in Jaris's car at the end of the day and asked, "What's hap'nin'?"

"I gotta get you home," Jaris replied. "Then I gotta pick up Sereeta at her grandma's. Sereeta and I are eating with Sereeta's stepdad tonight. Sereeta was nervous about going alone. I'm there for moral support."

"Perry Manley is gonna be outnumbered," Chelsea giggled. "Two against one."

"No, chili pepper," Jaris asserted. "it's not gonna be like that. We all gotta make nice so things are better at the house when Sereeta's mom gets home from rehab. She's gonna be fragile for a while. People being at each other's throats isn't gonna help the lady."

Jaris checked the e-mail on the computer, deleted most of it, and changed his clothes. He put on a nice white shirt and slacks. When Jaris arrived at Sereeta's grandmother's house, Bessie Prince sat in the parlor. Sereeta was still getting ready, and Jaris sat down opposite the older lady.

"That poor child is so tensed up," Bessie Prince commented. "It's a cryin' shame it has to be this way in families."

"It'll get better," Jaris consoled her, "when Sereeta's mother gets home from rehab." He wished Sereeta would hurry up so they could go. He was uncomfortable talking to her grandmother. He could feel her hostility against Olivia and Perry Manley.

Bessie Prince shook her head sadly. "I told you before, boy. I don't put much stock in people changing. I'm an old woman. I've known lots of folks for a good while. And they about the same when they old as when they were young. I go to church on Sunday and read the Good Book. I know it's all about sinners reforming and redemption, but I just ain't seen much of that in my life. I hope to heaven Olivia has changed her ways, but . . ."

Sereeta appeared then, wearing a pretty soft green sweater and dark slacks. She looked beautiful, as she always did. Jaris gave her a hug and a kiss.

As they walked out to the car, Sereeta remarked, "Grandma thinks this is all a waste of time."

"Yeah," Jaris nodded in agreement. "I got that."

"Maybe she's right, maybe not," Sereeta mused. "I mean, let's say Mom doesn't drink anymore. Then she and Perry can get on better." There was an underlying tone of desperation in Sereeta's voice. "I'll just have to make the best of it."

When they arrived at Angelo's, Perry's car was already there. He was driving a burgundy Jaguar.

"Your stepfather must be doing good," Jaris commented. "Nice wheels!"

"Yeah, he's doing well," Sereeta replied. "It costs a lot for Mom to be at that rehab place, and he's paying for everything. He really wants it to work."

Perry was sitting at a booth near the back. Sereeta walked a little ahead of Jaris.

When she got to the booth, she told Mr. Perry, "I hope it's okay that Jaris came. We've been friends for most of our lives. I texted you about it. You didn't text me back. So I figured . . ."

Perry Manley nodded toward Jaris. "Hello Jaris. It's fine that you're here." Manley looked weary, worried, hopeful. He also seemed to be glad Jaris was there.

When Jaris and Sereeta were seated, Manley looked at her. "It's been quite a ride, eh, Sereeta? A lot of water has gone over the dam," Manley sighed.

They all ordered salads. Even before their meals were served, Perry Manley got down to business. "Sereeta," he said, "like we said before, when we had that little talk. We don't have to like each other to get along, right?"

Sereeta nodded.

Manley went on in a calm tone. "I was thinking. When your mother gets home, we could have a regular time each week for a family dinner. Maybe Sundays or some other night. Whatever works for you, Sereeta. I'm not thinking one big happy family. But just a nice chance to get together on a regular basis. We'll never be the Cosby family but . . ." He smiled the best smile he could. "Sound okay to you, Sereeta?"

"Yeah, that's fine," Sereeta agreed.

"Jake is too young now to know much," Manley continued. "But as he gets older, it'd be nice if you two could be brother and sister. He *is* your half brother." Jake was the son of Sereeta's mom and Manley.

"Yes," Sereeta agreed, sincerely, "It would be nice."

"I'll be honest with you, Sereeta," Manley added. "I was very seriously thinking about divorcing your mother. I just couldn't take the drama anymore. I have a very demanding job, and my career means a lot to me. But now they're telling me that your mother is doing very well. She has a good chance of full recovery."

Perry Manley looked over at Jaris. "My wife suffers from depression, clinical depression. Some people freak at that, but . . ."

"No, sir, I understand it," Jaris responded. "My aunt takes medication for depression. It's just another illness. It's no different than taking medicine for kidney trouble."

"Exactly," Mr. Manley nodded, smiling. He continued to look at Jaris. "I understand you've been quite a rock in Sereeta's life, young man. I appreciate that. I know it hasn't always been easy for you. You're a fine young man."

Their meals came to the table. As they finished their salads, they exchanged small talk. Jaris felt Sereeta was maybe feeling better about her stepfather.

After paying the check, Mr. Manley looked at his watch. "I have a presentation I must give later," he announced. "So I must be going." He reached over and clasped Sereeta's hand. "I'm glad we got together," he told her. Then he shook hands with Jaris and left the restaurant. Through the window next to the booth, Sereeta and Jaris watched the burgundy Jaguar leave the parking lot.

"I think he's trying," Jaris commented.

"Yes," Sereeta agreed, "he's trying. And I will too."


On the way to school on Wednesday, Jaris wondered what Ms. McDowell might do about Lydell Nelson. He knew the teacher would never say anything to him or the other students. She religiously protected the privacy of all her students. She would never talk about one to another. Jaris knew she would try very hard to give Lydell any help he seemed to need. But she wouldn't violate his privacy either.

Later that day, Kevin Walker was crossing the Tubman campus at lunch time. He passed Lydell sitting on his stone bench and writing in his journal.

"Sometimes I got so much hate in me I feel like a pressure cooker," Kevin said aloud.

Lydell looked up and swiveled his head to see if anyone else was around.

Nobody. He said to Kevin, "Are you talking to me?"

"I'm just talking to the wind, man, but you can listen if you want," Kevin replied. Kevin turned and his dark eyes settled on Lydell. "You ever get mad at the world, dude?"

Lydell said nothing for a long moment. Then he closed his spiral notebook and put his pen in his pocket. Very quietly, he responded, "All the time."

Lydell did not invite Kevin to sit beside him on the bench. But there was plenty of room, and Kevin sat down. "It's just that the world is freakin' unfair, man," Kevin commented. "Real creeps seem to be flyin' high. Decent peeps are gettin' slammed all the time."

"Yeah," Lydell answered in a hushed voice. His eyes behind his glasses seemed to come alive in a strange new way. He looked like a miner who'd been digging for a long time and had finally struck gold. He was like an old prospector who'd been scratching in vain for half his life. Now he saw the glint of gold in the dirt.

"Sometimes I go to the gym. I whack the punching bag and spar with some guys," Kevin confided. "That helps. I run too. But the punching bag, that's the best. You ever do that, man?" Kevin asked, his dark eyes on Lydell again.

"No," Lydell replied.

"The old guy down at the gym," Kevin went on. "He's good about letting kids hang out there. He's a loser too. Lot more losers in life than winners, man. Life is like a pyramid, you hear what I'm sayin'? All the good stuff is at the top, but there's not much room there. Most of us down at the bottom scrambling for leftovers."

Kevin glanced over at Lydell to see if he making an impression. "Maybe I'll get serious about boxing. My old man was a good boxer. He was fixin' to go to the Olympics when he got in a fight and killed some dude. That was the end of him."

"Where's the gym at?" Lydell asked.

"About five miles down the highway," Kevin nodded. "I go there 'most every day after school. My grandfather lets me borrow his pickup."

"Charge much?" Lydell asked.

"It's freakin' free if you're still in high school," Kevin replied. "Old guy there's a good dude. Wanna go tomorrow with me?"

Lydell shrugged. "Maybe," he said. He didn't smile or show any expression. He went back to writing in his spiral notebook.

Kevin headed down toward the eucalyptus trees. For the past couple weeks, nobody had seen Carissa with Kevin. She used to come all the time. She was a pretty girl who wore her hair in corn rows. Jaris and Sereeta saw her in classes, and she seemed fine.

Nobody felt brave enough to ask Kevin Walker if he and Carissa had broken up. He had a hair-trigger temper, and a question like that could set him off. But Derrick

Shaw was there, eating the sandwich that his girlfriend, Destini, had made for him. Only Derrick was naïve enough to ask Kevin.

"Hey Kevin, what's with you and Carissa? I ain't seen you guys—" Derrick started to say. The smile on Derrick's face showed he didn't know he was stepping into quicksand.

"She's busy with her classes, and I'm busy too," Kevin snapped. A smart person would have let it go at that. But Derrick had a gift for speaking at the wrong time and saying the wrong thing. "You always have time for your lady," he blabbed on, "me and Destini—"

"MYOB, Derrick," Kevin growled. "You get my meaning?" He got up and stalked away, going up the trail and jogging across the campus.

"You sure walked into a buzz saw, Derrick," Jaris commented. "Lucky you didn't get a poke in the eye."

"What'd I say?" Derrick asked, a bewildered look on his face. "I was just wondering what happened to Carissa. They seemed so happy together."

Destini threw her arm around Derrick's shoulders. "You didn't say anything wrong, babe. It's just that somethin' went sour with Kevin and Carissa. He's been meaner than a pit bull with a sore paw lately."

"You think they broke up?" Derrick wondered, wide-eyed.

Sereeta had been looking down at the grass. She was plucking blades and slowly tearing them into shreds with her long fingernails. Now she asked, "You guys know Zendon Corman?"

"Yeah," Jaris replied. "He's the dude with the band. He's a senior. He put together this band in tenth grade, and it's gotten bigger and better. They play kind of an underground rave sound. Zendon is good-looking too."

"Well," Sereeta continued, "I think Carissa goes for that sound or something."

Alonee looked at Sereeta. "You saying Carissa dumped Kevin for Zendon?" she asked.

"Oh, I'm not saying that," Sereeta answered. "But she told me she really likes Zendon's music. Carissa got interested in Kevin right after he got to Tubman. He was really hot on the track team then. All the Twister mania, remember? Carissa likes guys who are getting a lot of attention. Right now, Zendon is kinda hot. His band does gigs at parties and stuff. Last month they did a little gig at the street fair."

"Oh brother!" Jaris moaned. He'd been noticing Kevin's mood was not so good lately. Jaris hadn't known what was at the bottom of it. Now he knew. They all knew. They sat there in silence under the eucalyptus trees.

# CHAPTER THREE

Zendon Corman called his band After the Crash. Sometimes he performed with two other guys from the neighborhood at a little club off Grant Avenue. New bands were allowed to perform and keep whatever change went into the bowl. Sometimes After the Crash performed for a small fee at small events.

Sami Archer had them play that Saturday night. She was throwing a fish fry celebrating her parents' wedding anniversary. Jaris and Sereeta were invited to the fish fry. When they walked in, Sami approached them with, "Hey, what's the scoop on Kevin and Carissa?"

Sereeta looked uncomfortable. "I think Carissa sorta likes Zendon Corman, Sami," she replied.

"She dumped Kevin?" Sami cried.

"I don't know, Sami," Sereeta responded. "Maybe they just both decided to see other people or something."

Jaris spotted Carissa then, near where Zendon was warming up with his band. Zendon was a tall guy with a big smile. He played the guitar and sang while the other guys played drums. He looked a lot happier than Kevin usually looked. Carissa was laughing with him.

"Plenty of fish and hot sauce," Sami was saying. "My daddy and my uncle got real lucky when they went fishin' yesterday. So eat up."

Jaris sampled some of the fish and washed it down with soda. He eased over to where Carissa was and asked, "Hey Carissa, wasup?" Oliver Randall and Derrick Shaw were right behind him.

"Aren't these guys awesome, Jaris?" Carissa bubbled. "Their music just gives me the chills."

"I'm kinda into soul now, Carissa," Jaris responded. "I'm listening to all kinds of music." Jaris paused then and said, "Uh Carissa, you and Kevin—?"

The smile left Carissa's face. She looked uncomfortable for a few moments. Then she said, "It got too tense with Kevin, Jaris. I was always like walking on eggs. You know those moods he gets."

"Oh yeah?" Jaris replied. "So then . . ."

"Yeah," Carissa admitted, "we were at this little club. I got to talking to Zendon, and Kevin got a little mad. We argued. I mean, Jaris, we're teenagers, right? I'm gonna be eighteen in a couple months. But anyway . . . that's too young to hang with just one guy all the time. Mom says I oughta be having fun with a lot of people. If Kevin is gonna get possessive . . ." Carissa looked sad. "It's not that I don't care about Kevin. I mean, *I do*, but . . ."

42

Jaris couldn't argue with Carissa's reasoning, but he felt sorry for Kevin. What if Sereeta suddenly started hanging out with some jerk with a band? He could only imagine how he would feel. Not that Kevin and Carissa had what Jaris and Sereeta had. But, still, Kevin seemed to like the girl a lot. They were always together.

"Kevin is going down to the gym a lot now, huh?" Jaris remarked. "I guess he thinks he might want to be a boxer."

"That's another thing I don't like, Jaris," Carissa responded. "I hate boxing. It's so brutal. We argued about that a coupla times. His dad was a boxer, you know. And it didn't help him control his violent streak. He ended up killing a guy. He ended up in prison and dying there in a riot. My mom says maybe Kevin has a violent streak too. Maybe he got it from his father in his genes or something. Mom's pretty smart. She reads a lot, and she watches this psychologist on TV. He talks about stuff like that. Sometimes Kevin scares me."

43

"Carissa, Kevin has never hit you or shoved you, has he?" Jaris asked.

"Oh no, never!" Carissa asserted. "He's a good guy, he really is."

Jaris had met Carissa's mother a few times. She was pretty, like Carissa. She dressed like a teenager. She didn't work. She just spent all day reading magazines and watching trash TV and gossiping with her friends. It was Carissa's mother who let Kevin's terrible secret leak—that his father had killed a man. That set up Kevin to be taunted by Marko Lane. Kevin almost went off the deep end. But Kevin forgave Carissa for revealing his secret to her mother. After all, Carissa *knew* her mother was a gossip. Kevin seemed to really love the girl to forgive her like that. Jaris felt very sorry about the whole thing. He wasn't mad at Carissa. She was confused. But he felt bad for Kevin. He deserved a break.

Jaris sat down under some trees in the Archers' yard and ate more fish with

Sereeta. "Usually I hate fish, but this sauce is great," he commented.

"Yeah, I love hot sauce. The hotter the better," Sereeta agreed.

The band stopped playing for awhile, and Zendon was sitting on the grass with Carissa. His hands were all over her. He bent over and kissed her, and she giggled.

"It's none of my business," Jaris noted, looking at the pair. "But that scene makes me sick."

"Yeah," Sereeta said. "But I guess a lot of teenaged romances break up."

"Except us," Jaris declared. "Remember our promise to each other? Someday we'd be sitting together in a little café in Paris. That'll be years from now, and we'll talk about the good old days. We'll love each other even more than we do now."

"That's impossible, Jaris," Sereeta smiled at Jaris.

"What's impossible?" Jaris asked her.

"That I could ever love you more than I do now," Sereeta replied, laughing. "You know, when we first started dating, I liked you a lot. But you liked me more than I liked you. Now I love you more than my own life."

"When we're sitting in that café in Paris," Jaris told her, "we'll talk about that play we were in, *A Tale of Two Cities*. And we'll talk about our friends and our teachers, Ms. McDowell and Mr. Pippin. And we'll talk about the crazy things like the Princess of the Fair contest, and going to the beach."

"We won't look like we do now," Sereeta mused. She reached up and ran her hand down the contours of Jaris's cheek. "You'll be older and wiser looking, but you'll still be handsome. You're the kind of guy who stays handsome all his life."

"And you'll still be beautiful, Sereeta," Jaris responded. "You'll always be beautiful. And I love you too, more than my own life, babe." He kissed Sereeta.

The next Monday morning at Tubman High, what Jaris feared would happen did happen. Many of the people at Sami's fish fry were kids from Tubman. They all saw Carissa and Zendon acting like sweethearts. The word was out that Carissa was hot for Zendon and that she was done with Kevin Walker.

Marko and Jasmine latched onto the news like flies on garbage. When Kevin showed up for Mr. Myers's English class, Marko was waiting for him.

"Hey dude, my condolences," Marko said with mock concern. "It's gotta be hard, man."

Kevin just glared at Marko and continued on his way to English. But Marko wasn't done. "She's really hot for Zendon now, you poor fool. She's left you in her dust. Hey, whatcha gonna do? That dude has a band. Chicks go for guys with bands. Maybe you oughta get yourself a band, dude."

Lydell Nelson was coming along and glanced in Marko's direction. He stopped in his tracks and stared blankly at Marko. It was as if an ugly little bug had wandered into Lydell's path.

"You ever see a man die?" Lydell asked Marko. Lydell's voice had no expression.

Marko looked startled. Jasmine gasped. "What's that?" Marko demanded. "Whaddya say, man?"

"I once saw two guys clobbering this man in the park," Lydell explained. "They just jumped him. I don't know why. He died."

Marko looked at Jasmine, then at Lydell. "Why you saying stuff like that to me, dude? You crazy? What's wrong with you saying stuff like that to me?"

Lydell shrugged and went into Mr. Myers's classroom.

"He one crazy dude," Marko said to Jasmine.

Kevin had watched the exchange without saying anything.

Later that day, when Jaris and Chelsea got home from school, Mom was sitting in the living room. Her principal, Mr. Greg Maynard, was there too. Mr. Maynard

had come to the Spain house for quite awhile.

For a long time, Jaris disliked Mr. Maynard. At that time, Mom and Pop had been fighting a lot. And he always seemed to be coming around. He was always showing up with his oily charm. He was divorced, and he clearly he liked Mom. Jaris always thought he wanted to cultivate a deeper friendship with her.

"Hello Jaris, Chelsea," Mr. Maynard called out when the pair came in. "My, you youngsters are growing." A huge smile was on his face. "You're a senior now, eh Jaris? And Chelsea, already going to Tubman High. Your mother tells me you're both doing very well."

Jaris felt he could never completely trust Greg Maynard. Like Mom and unlike Pop, he was educated, suave, and charming. He was also, Jaris thought, devious. Pop was just what he appeared to be. Mr. Maynard, Jaris thought, had hidden plans.

"I'm sure your mother has told you the exciting news," Greg Maynard gloated.

Jaris got nervous. He darted a look at his mother.

"Jaris, Chelsea," Mom explained, "I've been chosen to represent our school district at the convention in New Orleans next month. I'm just so very proud. Greg nominated me, but many other excellent teachers were nominated too. And I was selected! So I'll be spending four days in New Orleans planning the future of language arts education in our whole school system."

"Oh, that's great, Mom," Jaris said limply.

"You mean you'll be gone for four whole days?" Chelsea asked.

"Yes, sweetie," Mom chirped. "And I'm sure you guys can manage very well without me." Jaris had noticed that, when Greg Maynard was around, Mom chirped a lot. Jaris thought she sounded girlish and a little silly.

"We'll get to New Orleans on a Friday morning," Mr. Maynard added. "We'll be at the convention Friday, Saturday, Sunday, and Monday. We'll be returning Tuesday morning."

Jaris focused immediately on one little word—"we." Greg Maynard said, *"We'll* get to New Orleans." That meant Greg Maynard was going with Mom. "Were you chosen to represent the district too, Mr. Maynard?" Jaris asked.

Greg Maynard chuckled. "No, no. All the principals are going by virtue of their positions," he explained.

"When is this?" Jaris asked in an increasingly cold voice.

"In about four weeks," Mom replied. "I've never been to New Orleans. So that'll be exciting." Mom giggled. Mr. Maynard chuckled again.

"Everything about it will be exciting, Monica," Greg Maynard remarked.

To himself, Jaris said, "I bet it will. *I just bet it will.*"

Jaris wondered whether Pop knew about this yet. Surely Pop didn't know.

Pop went to work this morning whistling. He would not have done that if he knew about this. At the breakfast table, Pop was talking about the new uniforms he was getting for his auto repair business. They were going to be cool forest green uniforms. The logo "Spain's Auto Care" was going to be in black stitching on the pockets. Pop seemed on top of the world this morning. Business was booming at the garage. All was well.

Nope, Jaris thought, he doesn't know.

Jaris went down the hallway to his room, leaving Mr. Maynard and Mom talking in the living room. Chelsea followed closely.

"Jaris, that's bad, isn't it?" Chelsea said.

"The trip to New Orleans?" Jaris asked.

"Yeah. Both of them going is really bad isn't it?" Chelsea said again.

"It's not good," Jaris admitted.

"Pop doesn't know yet, does he?" Chelsea asked, a very serious look on her face. "He doesn't know she's going away with *him* for four days."

"Well," Jaris said. "It's not exactly just the two of them going someplace. It's a big teacher's convention. There'll be lots of people and seminars and stuff . . ."

"Pop won't like it," Chelsea declared.

"No," Jaris agreed. "You got that right, chili pepper."

"I wish she wasn't going," Chelsea sighed. "Things have been nice around here. I wish they hadn't chosen Mom."

"Yeah," Jaris responded.

Chelsea was quiet for a while. The wheels were turning in her head.

"Jaris," Chelsea asked grimly, "you know that fish fry we went to at the Archer house? Maya told me Carissa Polson has dumped poor Kevin for that skinny dude with the band. Zendon somebody? Carissa was just hanging out with Zendon and not meaning for anything to happen. Then pretty soon she decided she liked Zendon better than she liked Kevin."

Chelsea's eyes grew very large, and she looked worried. "Now Mom's gonna be hanging with that sneaky Greg Maynard, and he's real charming."

"No, no chili pepper," Jaris asserted. "That's not going to happen with Mom and Maynard. Mom loves Pop a lot, and she always will. It's different with Kevin and Carissa. You know Carissa. She's always been an airhead."

"But that old Maynard," Chelsea objected. "He likes Mom. He has this real gooey voice when he talks to Mom. He reminds me of a slippery snake."

"I don't like him either," Jaris admitted. "But I trust Mom. It's just a dull old teachers' convention, and it'll be over before we know it."

But in his heart, Jaris was having the same fears as Chelsea. He didn't want to upset his little sister even more, though, by agreeing with her.

"Pop won't like it," Chelsea said again. "Boy, it's gonna be bad around here tonight, Jare."

Jaris went to his computer and did some research for AP American History. But he couldn't concentrate. He heard Mom and Maynard in the living room. They were laughing and chatting and chuckling. Jaris hoped Maynard was gone by the time Pop came home. Jaris imagined Pop walking in, all greasy and sweaty, in his new green uniform. Then he'd see Maynard in his pressed suit, sitting on the sofa giggling with Mom.

Jaris shook his head. "Oh man, that would be one *bad* scene," he thought.

Jaris propped his chin in his hands. He'd read about New Orleans. It was a very romantic place. It had wrought iron balconies in the French Quarter and soft jazz floating from the windows. You could ride a riverboat down the Mississippi.

Luckily, Greg Maynard left about ten minutes before Pop came home. "Hey babe," he exclaimed to Mom. "You look beautiful as usual. I'd give you a big hug and kiss. But I'm in no condition to hug a beautiful lady right now." Pop laughed his big, hearty laugh. He was in a great mood.

"Oh Lorenzo," Mom bubbled, "something really exciting happened to me. About forty teachers were nominated to represent our school district at the big convention in New Orleans next month. And I was the one chosen!"

"Say again?" Pop asked.

"The big annual educational convention in New Orleans," Mom explained. The wind was slightly taken from her sails. She sounded nervous. "I was chosen over forty other teachers to represent our district."

Jaris and Chelsea stood in the hall, unseen and listening. They stiffened, waiting for Pop's response. Pop didn't respond.

"Next month," Mom went on. "The educational convention . . ."

"You goin' to New Orleans next month?" Pop asked.

"Yes, for four days," Mom explained. "I'll leave on a Friday and be back Tuesday morning. It's all expenses paid. It's quite an honor to have been chosen, Lorenzo. It'll look good on my teaching record."

"So, you goin' by yourself, Monie?" Pop inquired.

"Well, Mr. Maynard, my principal, of course, will be going too," Mom replied. "All the principals are going." Her voice had begun to sound hollow. It had lost its emotion.

"Mr. Maynard," Pop repeated in a hiss. "So the deal is, you and Maynard are goin' to New Orleans for four days." Pop's voice had turned rough at the edges. Jaris could only imagine the look on Pop's face. He didn't want to see it. Of such looks night- mares are made.

"Lorenzo, don't put it like that," Mom chattered with a shaky laugh. "We're both going to the educational convention in New Orleans. There will be hundreds of educa- tors from all over the country. We'll have seminars and workshops on the language arts programs in all the elementary schools. It's quite a big deal."

"And then, of course, there'll be time for a little recreation," Pop suggested. "Hey, all work and no play makes you teachers dull boys and girls. You hear what I'm sayin'? You guys'll get the chance to stroll through the French Quarter. You'll be serenaded by those dudes playing horns. Then maybe you'll stop at one of those little cafés. You know, where they got the lacy wrought iron balconies. Then you'll reach across the table and feed each other little shrimp canapés and stuff like that."

Pop's voice had moved from surprise, to annoyance, and now to raw hostility. It had not taken long. In the hallway, Jaris and Chelsea both leaned back slightly in fear.

"Lorenzo, I can't believe what I'm hearing," Mom gasped. "This is an honor. I've been chosen to make a contribution to the language arts programs throughout the country. I thought you'd be proud of me. Now you're turning this honor into some sleazy romantic getaway. For crying out loud, it's an educational convention!"

"Oh yeah, sure," Pop crowed. "But you gotta get away from all that boring talk about kiddie lit. Gotta just clear your heads. Maybe you'll want to take a lazy trip down the Mississippi, maybe in the moonlight. You could take one of those sternwheelers they got there, with guys standing on deck playing beautiful music. Oh that'll be nice. That'll be beautiful, Monie."

"I don't want to continue this ridiculous conversation," Mom announced. "If you are going to be childish about this, I'm just very disappointed. I didn't realize how immature you were. I thought you'd be proud of me. I was chosen over thirty nine other teachers—excellent teachers—to represent this district. We were all nominated by our principals for being the most outstanding teachers in a school, and I won. I should think you'd be congratulating me. Instead, you're carrying on like a child, like a jealous child."

"Yeah baby, I'm proud as punch," Pop growled. "Hey, it's like maybe I been chosen among all the other grease monkeys in town to go down to the car show. I get to hang with those babes in bikinis. Then like we'll all rendezvous down at the beach, the grease monkeys and the babes. We'll roast weenies and cavort around. Maybe swivel our hips dancin'. Now wouldn't that make you proud and happy, babe?"

"Lorenzo Spain, that is disgusting and insulting," Mom screamed. "I cannot believe you would sink so low. You're comparing an important educational convention with some beach party!"

Jaris leaned against the frame of his bedroom door, his forehead pressing into the wood. He closed his eyes and sighed. "Oh brother!" he moaned. Out of the corner of his eyes, he saw Chelsea. Her eyes were so wide they looked like dinner plates.

who's got better moves. If you know what I'm sayin'."

Mom sat there, looking as if she were being burned at the stake. Finally, she made an announcement. "My mother called today. She needed new eyeglasses. She had the worst time getting fitted, and the frames were all wrong for her."

"Oh hey," Pop responded, "now this is something we were all worried about. Everything's fallin' apart. Poor Kevin's getting two-timed by his chick. This Lydell guy goin' nuts writin' his thoughts in his journal. Stock market ain't so good neither. But Grandma Jessie got just the right glasses, so the world is all right after all." Pop cast a maniacal grin around the table. He'd be funny if he weren't so scary. He raised his water glass. "A toast to the old lady's new eyeglasses!"

Mom backed up her chair with a terrible grating sound. She stood up, almost upsetting the table and sending the rest of the pepperoni pizza to the floor. "I'm going to go work on the computer. I've had enough of this nonsense!" she cried.

"Hey, babe," Pop suggested, "'s long as you're on the computer, check out some of the hot tourist sites in New Orleans. You guys don't want to miss nothin'. Too bad you ain't goin' over there in the Mardi Gras. That'd be a hoot. You and Maynard could sashay down the street in grass skirts and masks, tearing up the old town."

Mom fled toward the computer.

Jaris and Chelsea both escaped to their rooms, supposedly to study.

Sitting in his room, Jaris felt whupped. This weekend the big event was supposed to be Olivia Manley's coming home. Her sister was driving her from the rehab center, and a little homecoming party was scheduled at the Manley home. It would be very low-key, with only close friends. Jaris and Sereeta would be there. And Monica Spain and Dawna Lennox, both Olivia's girlhood friends, were invited.

Perry Manley said he just wanted a small, warm group, not something that would overwhelm his wife on her first day home. He just wanted some cheerful talk and a little cake and ice cream. The people at the rehab center told Manley that his wife should slowly get back into her routine.

But now, with the turmoil over Mom's trip to New Orleans, Jaris's mind was on other things—his mom, his dad, and this stupid convention. He was struggling to focus on Sereeta's needs and her mother's. But he would have to, for Sereeta's sake.

At school the next day, Jaris told Sereeta about his mother's being chosen to represent the district at the New Orleans convention. He told her the principal of her school, Greg Maynard, would be going too. Sereeta knew the background on Maynard, and she frowned. "Wow, what an honor for your mom, but your dad can't be too thrilled."

"That's putting it mildly," Jaris agreed. "Last night at our house, it was war. Pop really has it in for Mom's principal. He's this sophisticated, good-looking dude, and he really likes Mom. He's divorced, you know. I don't think he'd mind making a play for Mom even though she's married."

"But she *is* married, Jaris," Sereeta asserted. "And I think he respects that. Besides, he's her superior. You know how it is today when bosses put pressure on women who work for them. This guy would be risking his whole reputation and his job."

"Yeah, you're right," Jaris admitted. "But Pop is gonna be freakin' out the whole time they're gone."

Just then, both Jaris and Sereeta swiveled their heads sharply. Marko Lane was racing toward them. Both Lydell Nelson and Kevin Walker were in hot pursuit. Marko had something in his hand. It looked like a page torn from a spiral notebook. Lydell wasn't a fast runner. But Kevin caught up to Marko and slammed him onto the grass, ripping the paper from him. Lydell arrived then, gasping for breath from the run. Kevin handed him the piece of paper.

As Marko was slowly getting up, Jaris and Sereeta and several other students trotted over to the scene.

"What's goin' on?" Jaris asked.

Marko was brushing grass clippings off his jeans, and he was furious. "That freak Nelson is up to something," he raged. "I grabbed a page from his stupid notebook. I wanna find out what we're up against before he goes nuts. I did it just to protect us from that wacko."

Kevin glared at Marko. "When I had you down, I shoulda punched your lights out, you moron," he sneered.

Lydell was putting the torn page in his binder, his face twisted with rage. "He just jumped me and tore a page from my notebook," Lydell fumed. "He had no right to do that. That's my private stuff. He had no right!"

"We gotta find out what this creep is up to," Marko declared. "I saw the title. It's

*Manifesto of the Doomed.* What does that sound like, you fools? You want to wait until he goes off and it's too late?"

"It's my stuff," Lydell asserted. "I'm not bothering anybody. You got no right to take my stuff."

Mr. Langston Myers approached. He had been passing by when Kevin tackled Marko and retrieved the paper. Now he strode over. "What's going on here?" he demanded. "We do not tolerate fighting on the campus."

"No fighting here, Mr. Myers," Kevin replied. "Marko Lane here, he snuck up behind Lydell and ripped a page from his journal. Then he ran off with it. I got the page back for Lydell."

Mr. Myers looked at Marko sternly. "Why would you do that, Mr. Lane?" he asked. "It is totally unacceptable behavior to violate the privacy of another student. Man up, Mr. Lane. You are a senior. What's wrong with you? Little kids sneak up on each other and grab their coloring books.

But we don't expect that sort of behavior from people who are almost adults."

"You don't understand, Mr. Myers," Marko objected. "Nelson is writing in that journal all the time. I think he's crazy. I think he's planning to do something bad around here. I was thinking about our safety, Mr. Myers."

Mr. Myers turned to Lydell. "Mr. Nelson," he inquired, "have you ever threatened anybody around here?"

"No, sir," Lydell responded. "I just write stuff in my journal for my own self."

"You were talking about a man being whupped to death in the park," Marko said accusingly.

"Yes, I saw that," Lydell replied. "I write about things I see and feel. It's for myself."

"You know what he wrote on the top of the page?" Marko cried. "*Manifesto of the Doomed*. What about *that*?"

"Mr. Lane," Mr. Myers sighed, "I've had about enough of you. In the short time you have been in my class, you have made yourself very easy to dislike. *Never* touch the property of another student. Do you hear me?"

"Okay, yeah," Marko agreed. He was afraid of Mr. Myers. This teacher was no pushover like poor Mr. Pippin, but even Mr. Pippin eventually got to the point that he cracked down on Marko.

Mr. Myers strode away then, carrying his splendid briefcase.

When the teacher was gone, Lydell turned to Kevin. "Thanks, man," he said quietly. "Nobody never stood up for me before in my whole life. Thank you." With that he walked away, clutching his journal.

"No wonder Carissa Polson dumped you, Walker," Marko taunted. "You're a freak!"

Kevin said something very softly. Only Jaris heard it. "Too bad," Kevin had mumbled, "that homeless guy who whacked you over the head with the baseball bat didn't do a better job." Everyone in the school knew what had happened to Marko. He'd been jogging at night. A homeless guy and his shopping cart got in Marko's way. Marko shoved the cart into the ravine—along with all the man's possessions. The man got so angry that he hit Marko in the head with a bat.

Jaris ignored Kevin's remark. If Kevin could let off steam saying things like that, it was better than teeing off Marko.

At one o'clock on Saturday, Jaris picked up Sereeta and drove to the Manley house. Jaris's mother and Dawna Lennox had driven together, and they were already there. "Mom and Dawna Lennox always got on good with your mom, Sereeta," Jaris commented. "I know she's glad to see them."

When Sereeta and Jaris walked into the living room, everyone was having coffee.

Jaris's mother looked up and asked, "You kids want sodas?"

"Coffee is fine, Mom," Jaris replied.

Sereeta hurried over to the ornate chair where her mother sat and gave her a hug and a kiss. "Mom," she exclaimed, "you look beautiful."

Olivia Manley smiled broadly. "I feel wonderful, sweetheart. We just got home about thirty minutes ago. My sister and her dear husband dropped me off here. Then they had to run and get back home to their own teenagers. Monie and Dawna were already here helping Perry make coffee. And, of course, they brought these delicious little cookies."

Her gaze swept Dawna Lennox and Monica Spain. She looked wistful for a moment. A generation ago they were three young girls giggling together. That all seemed eons ago.

"You girls were always my best friends," Olivia Manley said to Monie and Dawna. "Remember how we almost flunked chemistry with Ms. Winslet? All but you Monica. You were a whiz."

Dawna Lennox laughed.

"Oh it's *so* good to be home," Sereeta's mother announced. "They were wonderful to me at the place but . . ."

Olivia Manley wore a floral blouse and slacks. She looked better than she had looked in a long time. Jaris could not remember her looking so good. He was used to seeing her weary and wasted looking. Now she was radiant and healthy. And she was bubbling over with plans.

"Perry kept busy arranging for the landscaping of that new development in the city," she reported. "We passed it on the way home. Just enchanting. Lovely drought-resistance plants, colored stones. Magical. You're a genius, darling! No wonder you're doing so well."

The woman turned to Sereeta then. "Perry has been telling me how you're coming here for dinner every week, sweetheart. We'll all be together at last. Thursday is just perfect. That will be so nice—me and you, Perry, and little Jake."

"Yeah," Sereeta affirmed, "I can come early and make dinner for us. I've learned a lot about cooking since I'm living with grandma. There's this one dish I make, stuffing-topped pork chops with cream-style corn. It's just awesome. Grandma say it's the best thing she ever tasted. Grandma and I just love it."

"Your grandmother is quite a heavy-weight," Perry Manley chimed in. "At least she was the last time I saw her. Obesity is quite a problem today, but it's worse for some of us African Americans. You might want to make a healthier dish, Sereeta."

Jaris winced but said nothing. Even if Perry Manley felt that way, he shouldn't have said so like that. He insulted the grandmother whom Sereeta loved. Of course, he didn't like the grandmother because she was the mother of Olivia's first husband. Jaris took a quick glance at Sereeta. A shadow of hurt flashed in her eyes, but she recovered quickly. She was determined to let nothing rain on her mom's homecoming. "Well, then how about if I make nice apricot-glazed pork on rice. That's yummy and very low in fats."

"Sounds wonderful, sweetheart," Olivia Manley said. "My, it's so amazing to hear my little girl talking about making fancy meals."

Looking about the room, she sighed and remarked, "What a lovely day this is."

"You better get some rest now, dearest," Perry Manley suggested. He looked at the two women and at Jaris and Sereeta. "Thank you so much for coming. Let's hope this is the beginning of a happy new chapter for all of us."

Monica Spain and Dawna Lennox cleaned up the dishes quickly. They then hugged Olivia and went out together. Sereeta and Jaris were standing by his car.

"She really does look good, Sereeta," Monica Spain remarked, as the four of them stood on the sidewalk.

"Yes," Dawna Lennox agreed. "I hope Perry tries really hard to keep stress out of her life."

"I'm going to try hard too," Sereeta declared. "Every time my stepfather used to say something that hurt my feelings, I'd strike back or I'd hold a grudge. I'm not doing that anymore. The important thing is for Mom to stay well. I know I'll never really like Perry, but I can pretend for Mom's sake. I really can."

Jaris and Sereeta got into the car and drove off. They were planning a quick swim in the ocean before going home. They both needed the relaxation. Today had been stressful for Sereeta. She had not known quite what to expect. And Jaris was thinking about what was going on at home with that trip to New Orleans coming up.

The hot, muggy days of early fall were waning. Soon it would be too chilly to swim in the ocean and lie on the beach and enjoy the cool wind blowing over their wet bodies. But today Jaris and Sereeta raced into the water like carefree children, splashing each other and screaming and laughing. For just this little while, on perhaps the last good hot day of summer, they enjoyed the pleasure of the refreshing water.

After their swim, Jaris and Sereeta lay on their beach towels.

"I know I should be happy that Mom got that great honor to represent our school district," Jaris admitted. "But Pop is so upset. Pop's a great guy. But when something rubs his fur the wrong way, boy, it's not nice around the house."

"Yeah. Well, at least he's up front about it," Sereeta responded. "Lots of guys would tell their wife how happy they are and then they'd sulk. Or they'd get back at them in sneaky ways. One of the things I love about your dad is you know just where you stand with him."

"You know, though," Jaris explained, "Pop has always kinda felt inferior to Mom. She has a college education, and he doesn't. And she's very professional and stuff like that. Having the garage now has helped him a lot. But he sees that Greg Maynard is more in Mom's league. You know what I mean? Professional . . . well dressed . . . he's sorta the opposite of Pop."

Jaris was quiet for a moment before he went on. "It just burns Pop up to think Mom and that guy will be there in New Orleans. Maynard is always buttering Mom up, telling her how wonderful she is. Pop, well, he loves Mom like crazy, but he's not Mr. Charm, you know?"

"Jaris, your parents are so in love with each other that it's amazing," Sereeta told him.

"I know they love each other. I've seen them in the kitchen at night, dancing around, their arms around each other. Still, I look at the two of them sometimes from the outside. Greg Maynard is the kind of guy you'd think Mom would have married."

"But she didn't, Jaris," Sereeta insisted, "and therein lies the tale. They're the real deal, babe. Trust me. I've spent my whole life seeing what was not the real deal. I know the real deal, and your parents are it."

# CHAPTER FIVE

On Monday afternoon, Jaris dropped Chelsea at Inessa Weaver's home. Athena Edson, Falisha Colbert, and Keisha were already gathered there for a sleepover. They were going to watch a movie on Inessa's family's big new screen. Then they were going to pile into Inessa's big bedroom and sleep on the floor in sleeping bags. They wouldn't do much sleeping, though, if the past was any sign of how things would go. At the last sleepover at the Spain house, the girls talked until three in the morning. The conversation was interspersed with wild laughter that kept Jaris awake all night. Luckily for the Weaver family, Tuesday was a teacher's workday at Tubman. The kids had the day off. Inessa's parents planned to bring all the girls home about midmorning after a pancake breakfast.

Pop wasn't home when Jaris pulled into the driveway. Since he'd hired Darnell Meredith, he was coming home earlier. The two men got their work done quicker. It wasn't like it used to be when Pop worked for old Jackson, who did very little work. Pop had to do the lion's share of the auto repairs, and he often came home in the dark. Now two good mechanics were on the job: Pop who was terrific and Darnell who was very good. They made a hard-working team. But today Pop wasn't home, and Jaris had a sinking feeling. He figured Pop's not coming home had something to do with New Orleans. The convention coming up next month was on Pop's mind twenty-four-seven.

When Jaris went in the house, Mom was on the computer. She looked up over her shoulder and smiled glowingly. "I'll be giving several presentations at the convention. I'm polishing them up. You know we instituted that new language arts program here. Now we've got the chance to share what we learned with the whole country."

"Yeah, that's good, Mom," Jaris replied half-heartedly.

Mom turned herself around in the office chair and put her hands on her knees. "Jaris," she said, looking at him directly, "I'm really sorry about how your father is acting. It must be upsetting to you and your sister. I'm really sorry. I don't know what the man expects me to do. Greg and I can really make an important impact on education for our kids. Your father's selfish concerns can't stand in the way. He's acting like a spoiled child."

Jaris had been on his way to his room. But he turned to face his mother when she began to speak to him. He went back into the living room, sitting down. "Well, you know Mom," he responded, "this Maynard dude . . . I don't like him that much either."

"*What*?" Mom demanded. "What are you talking about, Jaris? Everybody likes and admires Greg at school."

"Mom," Jaris squirmed a little as he spoke. "Guys like him, they're devious. They're phony. Behind the smiles and the chuckles, they got their agenda."

"Now you're sounding almost as ridiculous as your father! What is Greg's 'agenda'?" Mom demanded.

"He likes you, Mom. He likes you too much," Jaris told her.

Mom gasped. "Jaris! Are you out of your mind? Greg has never been inappropriate with me. Never!"

"Mom, he's got his eyes on you. That's what worries Pop," Jaris insisted.

"This is so unbelievably ridiculous," Mom stormed. "I have a strictly professional relationship with Greg Maynard. He is my boss. To read anything else into it is *sick*. I can't believe your father's unfound jealousies appear plausible to you, Jaris."

"Like Carissa at school, dumping Kevin," Jaris explained. "She just got carried away. It can happen with guys and chicks."

"I'm disappointed in you, Jaris," Mom scolded. "Your father's poisonous Neanderthal thinking has seeped into your brain." Mom looked suddenly stricken by her own choice of words. She hadn't meant to call Pop a "Neanderthal."

Jaris looked silently at his mother. After a moment of embarrassed silence, Mom said, "I didn't mean to use that word, Jaris, and you know it. Don't be looking at me like that. You have that aggrieved look on your face. You're thinking I'm insulting your poor suffering father who has every right to want me to turn down this wonderful opportunity. And you think I should do that just because of his absurd concerns."

Mom's voice quivered with emotion. She had suspected for a long time that her son and daughter, especially Jaris, were more their father's children than hers. No matter how off the wall Pop was, Jaris tended to take his side. The thought was maddening to Monica Spain.

"Jaris," Mom said, trying to defend herself, "remember that argument about putting another big mortgage on our home so your father could buy the garage? He won that argument. I had horrible misgivings, yet I gave in."

"I know, Mom and it's working out terrific," Jaris admitted. "Pop is doing great. He's like increased business at the garage by over thirty percent. I went over his spread sheets with him, and it was amazing. Before Pop took over, the garage was dirty, and Jackson wasn't always too efficient. The reason more customers are coming in is because Pop has streamlined and cleaned up the place. Pop was right about buying the business."

"Yes, and I was wrong," Mom conceded bitterly. "Just as I am *always* wrong in your eyes."

Jaris felt as if he'd hurt his mom badly. He wanted desperately to make her feel better.

"No, Mom," he told her, "I think you have to go to the convention in New Orleans. You'll do a great job. I'm proud that you were chosen to represent all the teachers around here. It's a great honor, and you deserve it. It's just that you're all the time talkin' about Maynard—'Greg this' and 'Greg that.' It sounds like you guys are too close. I wish you'd just cool that part, you know."

Mom was listening, and Jaris went on. "I *know* Pop is too jealous. And I know you've never given him any reason to be that way. But, Mom, *he loves you so much.* You know, most of my friends—their parents aren't married anymore. Trevor's mom is single. Oliver's parents are friends but they hardly see each other except in the summer. Sereeta's family is a disaster. I mean, I'm so grateful that I got parents like you guys. I don't want anything to, you know . . ."

Jaris couldn't come right out and express his darkest fears.

"Honey," Mom said softly, "I love the man I married with all my heart. I always will. Even when I want to strangle him, I love him even then. This is never going to change. Greg Maynard is a nice man, and he's wonderful to work for. He happens to make my job easier. But he means nothing to me in any other way. Nothing."

"I know, Mom," Jaris admitted. But he still felt anxious about the trip to New Orleans and how it was upsetting Pop. Jaris wanted to say more. But what could he say that wouldn't hurt Mom more?

"You comin'?" Kevin Walker asked Lydell Nelson after English class on Wednesday.

Lydell stuffed his journal into his backpack and followed Kevin to his pickup in the parking lot. The rusty pickup sat waiting like a patient old horse. Kevin borrowed it from his grandfather

They drove to Eddie Gerkin's gym, north of the Grant neighborhood. It was in a rundown area where graffiti was scrawled on every fence and wall. Once factories hummed in the area, and hundreds of people had work. But now most of the buildings were abandoned.

Concrete steps led up to the gym. Kevin sprinted up, two steps at a time, but Lydell went slowly. He weighed too much. He'd weighed too much since he was nine. His father weighed too much too. His dad never told Lydell how to eat properly. They both lived on burgers and fries. Lydell was happy in those days. He stopped being happy when he was ten, and he was never happy since then.

Eddie Gerkin had once trained good fighters. One of his boys won the welterweight championship. Lately, though, most kids were more interested in other sports: martial arts, soccer, extreme sports. But boxing was still Eddie's life. He was a sixty–something African American with white hair. He'd met Lydell when Kevin brought him the first time. He thought the kid looked lazy.

The gym smelled bad—too many sweating bodies. Kevin didn't notice. A pretty black girl was boxing in one of the rings. Kevin looked at her for a few moments. Then he and Lydell walked toward the heavy bags that hung on chains from the ceiling.

Eddie wrapped the boys' hands, and then they put on gloves. Lydell was terrible at first, but then he got the hang of it.

"Name the bags," Kevin advised Lydell. "You're not hittin' the bag. Your hittin' your demons. It's Marko Lane. Bam, bam, bam. Doesn't that feel good, man?"

The heavy bag Lydell was whacking away at began to swing. As he hit it harder, the bag swung more. Lydell smiled a little. Kevin never saw him smile before.

"That's it, dude," Kevin urged him.

Kevin skipped backward from the bag, practicing footwork. As he did, he glanced over at the girl in the ring. She had short, curly hair and big shoulders for a girl. Her arms were toned. She was pretty. Kevin kept looking at her from time to time.

After a while, Lydell stepped back from the bag.

"How often you come here?" Lydell asked Kevin.

"Pretty much every day after school, when I don't have track practice. I do stretching, shadowboxing. I hit the bags a lot," Kevin answered.

"You said your father was a fighter," Lydell said. "He still around?"

"No," Kevin replied. "He got in a fight with another guy and killed him. They sent Pa up, and he died in prison."

"My father's gone too," Lydell admitted.

"Dead?" Kevin asked, his gaze still on the girl boxer. Her muscles flexed. She had great moves. She sparred with a guy, dancing and jabbing like a pro. All the while, she kept her right hand up. When she connected, she made a pop-pop-pop sound.

89

"Yeah," Lydell replied. He was poking at the bag every now and then, but not really punching hard. "We were in the park. We'd stopped for burgers like usual. Some guys came along. They started hitting my father. I don't know why. I got scared and ran. I hid. I thought they'd beat me up too. They whupped on him like crazy, laughing and stuff. Then they went away. I went over to my father. I'm goin', 'Hey Pa, you okay?' But he didn't say anything. He looked awful. His whole face was split open . . ."

Lydell was sweating now, as profusely as the girl in the ring. "I screamed and people came. Cops too," Lydell went on.

"Was he dead?" Kevin asked, turning to look at Lydell.

"Yeah. I saw it happen," Lydell nodded as he spoke. "I didn't do anything. I just ran and hid, and I didn't do anything" Lydell's voice was heavy with grief. "He was my pa, and he was good to me. I shoulda done something."

Kevin's full attention was on Lydell now. He asked, "How old were you, man?"

"Ten," Lydell answered.

"What could you do, man?" Kevin assured him. "A ten-year-old kid against a gang of grown men. You're lucky to be alive yourself."

"Sometimes I dream about it," Lydell continued. "I'm there in the park. I grab a branch from a tree. I go after them and smash them, and my father isn't dead anymore. He gets up from the grass, and he's okay."

"Nothin' you could do, man," Kevin asserted. "You live with your ma now?"

"It was just Pa and me," Lydell explained. "Ma died when I was four. It was just him and me. He was a good dad. I think he was the best dad any kid could have."

"They catch the guys who did it?" Kevin asked.

"No," Lydell answered. "Cops said they were drunk. Drunk and mean. One of them said, 'Let's whup fatso.' I remember hearing that. They thought it was funny. It's been a long time. It's what they call a cold case now."

"So where you livin' now, man?" Kevin asked.

"With my aunt," Lydell replied. "My ma's sister. She doesn't like it. She's got kids. She don't need me."

Kevin watched the girl in the ring again. Her punches were sharp. She was really good. She moved from side to side, her body like a dancer's.

"Kevin, I never told anybody about what happened to my pa," Lydell confided.

"If you're wondering if it's safe with me, dude, don't worry," Kevin assured him. "It won't go no farther than us. I swear."

Kevin meant what he said. After all, he had the secret about his dad, who died in prison. Kevin knew how Lydell was feeling.

"Lydell, man," Kevin nodded toward the ring. "Look at that chick. She's got good combinations. What a babe."

"Yeah," Lydell agreed. But he wasn't looking at her.

The girl left the ring and went to join a group of friends. Kevin called out to her, "You're sharp, babe."

The girl smiled at him.

"I'm not good with people," Lydell confided. "That's why I write so much. I feel safe when I do that."

"I'm kind of a loner myself, Lydell," Kevin admitted. "I had a girlfriend, but she quit on me. Found somebody she liked better."

The girl boxer stood talking with a couple guys and another girl. She turned and looked back at Kevin. She seemed to like the looks of the tall, dark-eyed young man.

She pointed toward Kevin and Lydell. "You guys wanna go for hot dogs? There's a little dive down the street that caters to people like us." She laughed.

Kevin looked at Lydell, who seemed nervous. "Yeah, sure," Kevin called back. "I never met a hot dog I didn't like."

"We're driving a red Ford," the girl boxer told him. "You can follow us."

"You got it!" Kevin confirmed.

They ended up at a small diner, where they all squeezed into a booth.

"Funny to see a chick boxing," Kevin told the girl.

"Lotta girls boxing now," the girl retorted. "Hey, I'm Rochelle Bailey. My sister, Lia. My friend, Lou. You guys in college?"

"Seniors at Tubman," Kevin replied.

"I just graduated Lincoln," Rochelle offered. "I'm in community college. I want to be a personal trainer or something."

"You look great boxing, girl," Kevin told her.

"I'm gonna be in a three-rounder tomorrow. Be wearin' headgear," Rochelle announced, looking at Kevin. "What do you want to do with your life?"

"Maybe be a boxer too," Kevin smiled. "Maybe someday we'll be in a match, you and me."

The hot dogs were good. And, Kevin thought, the company was better.

As they drove through the darkness on the way home, Lydell spoke up. "It was fun at the gym. You're right, Kevin. It lets the stress out a little."

"Yeah, it does," Kevin affirmed.

"Rochelle seemed interested in you, Kevin," Lydell remarked. "She kept looking at you."

"I was lookin' at her too," Kevin said.

"You said before you had a girlfriend, but she went for some other guy," Lydell commented. "You hate her for that?"

Kevin didn't answer right away. His fingers tightened on the wheel, and Lydell could see his veins popping out on the backs of his hands. "Me and Carissa were doing good," Kevin answered. "Then she heard this dude singing with his creepy band, and she sort of drifted off. He came on to her. Me and Carissa been together for a while. It hurt when she took off. And yeah . . . I kinda hate her."

"Maybe she'll get sick of the other dude and come back," Lydell suggested.

"I wouldn't have her back," Kevin said.

"People are hard to figure," Lydell remarked. "That's why I try to stay away from them. Like my aunt. She lets me live there, but she wishes I wasn't there. She's got kids, my cousins. One of them is about my age. He bullies me. He snaps his fingers in my face and hurts my lips. Then he laughs. He says if I say anything, I'm outta there. So I just take it."

"That's a bad deal, dude," Kevin responded sympathetically. "I live with my grandparents. They're good people. They're real old, and they got health problems. But they do their best. When I was a kid, we'd all go camping together, me and Mom and the grandparents. I got to love them a lot. I see my grandfather getting slower now. He's hurtin' in his joints, and it makes me sad. Life ain't easy, man. The people you hate make your life miserable, and the people you love make you worry."

"I wish I had a lot of money so I could pay my aunt what she's spent on me and then get out of there," Lydell said. "I'd never look back."

"I hate real easy," Kevin responded. "There's a couple kids at school I feel good about. There's this group, they call it Alonee's posse for this chick Alonee Lennox. She brought everybody together. I like those guys—Jaris, Oliver, Derrick, Sami, and Sereeta, Jaris's chick. I like being with them. I don't talk much. But we go down under the eucalyptus trees for lunch, and they're jabbering away. I just lie on the grass and look at the clouds. Nobody bugs me. If you want to join us, just come. You can write in your journal and nobody cares. That's how they are."

Kevin dropped Lydell home. Then he went to his grandparents' house. He was a little late. As he neared the house, he saw the bent figure of his grandfather in the doorway, watching for him.

# CHAPTER SIX

On Thursday, Jaris was walking toward the lunch spot under the eucalyptus trees. Then he spotted Zendon, walking with a tall, pretty girl he did not recognize. Jaris did a double take. Zendon and the girl seemed very affectionate toward each other. At one point, they stopped, and Zendon leaned over and kissed her. As Jaris drew closer, he heard the girl say, "I just think the grunge bands were awesome. I mean, they were before my time, but I've got all the music. Your stuff is so fresh, Zen. But it reminds me of the best grunge ever. It's your own sound, but it's eerie."

Zendon laughed. In some weird way, he sounded like Greg Maynard. Maynard chuckled and laughed a lot too when he and Mom were talking. It was his way of showing approval of what she was saying. He was showing delight in all her wonderful ideas. He'd go, "Monie, why didn't I think of that? You're *amazing*!"

Jaris never liked Zendon, and he didn't like Greg Maynard either. When Jaris got down by the trees, he saw his friends—Sereeta, Alonee, Oliver, Destini, Derrick, and Carissa. He was really surprised to see Carissa. She hadn't been coming since she broke up with Kevin. Kevin kept coming alone, but then he sort of dropped out too.

"Hi, you guys," Carissa greeted. She seemed a little nervous, sitting down quickly. She opened her carton of yogurt, peeling off the top and licking it. "Lemon, my fave," she remarked.

"How you been, Carissa?" Derrick asked. "You been a stranger for a while."

"Oh . . . I just had stuff to do at lunchtime," Carissa explained. Suddenly she looked very sad.

Sami Archer came down the trail and declared, "Well, look who's here. The little lost sheep has returned!"

"I missed you guys," Carissa admitted. "I . . . uh . . . miss Kevin a lot too. I mean, we had this stupid argument. I was listening to Zendon's music, and I guess Kevin got the wrong idea. Well, I mean, I hung with Zendon for a while, but he's not for me. I wish I'd never done it. Kevin gets mad so easy. I mean, I never stopped caring about him but . . ." She looked around hopefully. "He still comes here, doesn't he? I mean . . . to have lunch with the gang?" There was hope in her eyes.

"No child," Sami replied, "he ain't been coming lately. He got a new friend now, and they hang up on the stone benches."

Carissa's pretty eyes widened. "A girl?" she asked.

"No," Sami shook her head. "He been hangin' with that strange dude, Lydell Nelson. He the one all the time writin' in his book, like he's a spy or somethin'. Like he takin' down notes about us." Sami laughed. She didn't really think Lydell was a spy.

"Oh," Carissa sighed, relieved. "I just thought if I came down here, I'd run into Kevin. I mean, we were really tight you know. I thought if I explained to Kevin that it really wasn't any big deal with Zendon . . . I just sorta liked his music, and one thing led to another."

Jaris thought about what was happening in his own house. It was just like what happened to Kevin and Carissa. Mom liked and admired Greg Maynard. As Mom often said, it was no big thing. But maybe Greg Maynard would come on strong when they got to New Orleans. Maybe something would happen, and everything would change forever. Louisiana moonlight would work its magic.

Jaris knew he was letting his imagination run away with him again. He hated himself when he did that. He was going down that dark path again, where he feared all was going wrong. Jaris found it all too easy to get lost in the onrushing darkness. That's why he understood Pop. His father knew that darkness too, and it sometimes overwhelmed him. Mom was sunshine and light, and she never felt the darkness.

"Tell you what, child," Sami suggested. "Kevin been real moody lately. That dude is hangin' with Lydell, and they fightin' their demons together. Y'hear what I'm sayin'? They kinda found each other in the dumps. Now they go down to some ratty old gym and punch bags. They let the anger out like that. Kevin kinda like a buzz saw right now. You best stay clear of the boy till he settles down."

Carissa looked hurt. "Just 'cause I enjoyed some other guy's music and told him so? That's no reason for Kevin to hate me. I mean, I didn't do anything terrible." Carissa quietly finished her lemon yogurt. Then she left the spot under the eucalyptus trees in search of Kevin.

Kevin was sitting alone on the grass by the statue of Harriet Tubman when Carissa found him. He had just run around the football field, and he was getting his breath. Carissa approached him slowly, "Hi Kevin," she said.

"Hi," he replied in a flat voice.

"Kevin, I'm sorry if I hurt your feelings, but all I did was—" she began.

"Get lost," Kevin snapped, getting up from the grass.

"Kevin, I wasn't dating Zendon or anything. I was just—" Carissa stammered.

"Get lost, girl," he snapped again, brushing the grass off his running shorts.

"I didn't do anything," Carissa began to cry.

"Nothin' but kissin' up with that punk Zendon behind the oleander bushes by the gym," Kevin sneered. "Good old Jasmine Benson told me all about it."

"She's a liar!" Carissa gasped. "You'd believe that two-faced liar?"

"Yeah, I believed you for a long time, didn't I?" Kevin snarled, "Jaz saw what she saw and that's it. It's okay, babe. Don't sweat it. Just stay out of my way, okay? Everybody been talkin' about what's going on with you and Zendon. I'm sick of it. I wanted to punch Zendon out, but that was stupid. I thought, 'Hey, the dude did me a favor taking a chick like that off my hands.'"

"Kevin," Carissa wept, "I made a mistake, okay? Can't you forgive one little mistake?"

"Know what, babe?" Kevin said, standing squarely in front of Carissa. "We were juniors, and I confided in you. I told you the biggest secret of my life—that my pa was a murderer who died in a prison riot. You blabbed it to your mom, and she spread it all over the neighborhood. Marko Lane put me through hell because of that, but I forgave you. I forgave you, babe, 'cause you didn't do it on purpose. I forgive mistakes, not stuff like wrapping yourself around Zendon Corman. You blew it, girl. You can't lose what you never had, and we never had anything. So, like I said, get lost."

"Kevin, I thought you were better than this," Carissa wept.

Kevin looked right at the girl with near hatred in his eyes. "That makes two of us, babe. I thought you were better too." He turned then and walked away.

Carissa turned too, sobbing loudly. She ran across the campus. Alonee spotted her and ran after her. "Carissa, are you okay?" she called to the other girl.

Carissa kept on running. Jaris saw her and walked up to Alonee.

"What's that about?" he asked Alonee.

"I guess she and Kevin had it out. She's done with Zendon, and she wants to get back with Kevin. I guess he wasn't ready to be with her," Alonee said.

"I like Kevin," Jaris commented. "He's a good guy. But you don't cross the line with him. He's done a lot of favors for all of us, but he doesn't fool around. Carissa made a bad mistake. She stepped over the line. If she wanted to date another guy she just should have been up front about it. But she sneaked around and made a fool of Kevin."

"So you think he's right in not forgiving her, Jaris?" Alonee asked.

"Oh brother, who knows?" Jaris sighed. "Who knows anything anymore?"

As Jaris walked to his afternoon classes, Sereeta fell in step beside him. "Too bad about Carissa and Kevin," she remarked.

"Yeah," Jaris replied, "maybe they weren't a good match. Carissa went for Kevin when this Twister mania was all around the school. Remember? When Kevin first arrived at Tubman and turned out he could run like a Texas twister. Then Zendon got hot with his band, and she's gone to him. Maybe the girl needs to do a little growing up."

"It's kind of Kevin to be reaching out to Lydell Nelson," Sereeta said. "A lot of us reached out, but he got through."

"I bet Ms. McDowell very quietly and gently enlisted Kevin's help with Lydell,"

Jaris replied. "That's something she would do after we had our talk with her. She sees something in Kevin. She sees that he can help Lydell better than anybody else. She's got an amazing insight into people."

"When I was feeling so low," Sereeta responded, "she helped me so much. She told me something I'll never forget. I kinda borrow trouble. I worry and worry about what's going to happen down the line. It keeps me from being happy in the present. Ms. McDowell said, 'Sereeta, don't think about tomorrow.' Just a few simple words. Now, when I start to torture myself with what-ifs, I just remember those words. I don't think about tomorrow."

"I'm that way too," Jaris admitted.

"Yeah," Sereeta went on. "I'd be freakin' out before that first family dinner at the Manley house. But no, I refuse to do that. Grandma is making stuffed pork chops tonight with cream-style corn and sweet potato pie. And I'm gonna enjoy today with all my might. Then Grandma and I will watch her programs on TV. It'll be nice and peaceful."

After school, Lydell and Kevin went down to the gym again. Lydell didn't like the gym as much as Kevin did, but he really liked being with Kevin.

"You know, Kevin," Lydell remarked as they drove toward the gym, "I told you I never told anybody else about my pa dying like he did. I told you 'cause you seem as screwed up as I am. I thought you'd understand."

Kevin threw back his head and laughed. "You got that right, dude. I like those guys I hang with at Tubman, but none of them are like me. I mean, none of them as bad as me. I think I could kill Marko Lane, but none of them could. I won't kill him, or *anybody*. But I think I could. Those guys like Jaris and Oliver, they couldn't even imagine such a thing."

"I'm not strong enough to do somebody in," Lydell confided. "But I'd like to have hurt the guys who killed my pa. He was all

I had, man. He was a big, fat guy, and I looked up to him. I felt safe with him. I thought nobody could hurt me 'cause I was with my pa. We'd go fishing and to the amusement parks. We'd always be having fun, him and me."

Lydell stared out the truck's windshield. "He sold insurance," Lydell went on. "He was just an ordinary guy, but he was really big in my world. I lived in his shadow and when the shadow was gone I felt like I was naked before the world. For a long time, I just cried. Then one day I saw the light. And it was like I just started to write in my journal. Kevin, it's what keeps me from going crazy."

"I hear you, man," Kevin affirmed. "With me it's running and boxing. It's like all these demons are clawing at me. Then I bust out and run. I outrun them all. They're trying to catch me, but they can't. And in the gym, I'm beatin' on those bags. They're my demons, and I'm pulverizing them. Running and boxing. Like they save me."

Kevin looked over at Lydell. "Wackos like us, Lydell, we got to find an escape hatch in this insane world."

Lydell laughed a little. He didn't mind Kevin calling him a "wacko." Plenty of people called him that, and he hated the name. But with Kevin it was different. The thing that blew him away with Kevin was that Kevin said, wackos "like us." Lydell wasn't all alone anymore and being mocked for his strangeness. Now he had a partner. What Kevin said was like somebody giving him a hand when he was drowning. This cool, handsome athlete, Kevin "Twister" Walker, was comparing himself to pudgy little Lydell Nelson, who felt totally unloved and unwanted.

The major earthquake over Mom's upcoming trip to New Orleans had subsided. But in its aftermath, the family atmosphere had changed. No more did Pop try to make it home early. He no longer went into the kitchen to whip up one of his masterpieces for dinner. No more did Pop come home whistling and making jokes with Mom as soon as he entered the house. Pop was staying later at the garage. When he did come home, he wasn't very cheerful. That change in their dad's mood bothered Jaris and Chelsea a lot. It was great when Pop came home happy and bantered with everybody. They liked to see him and Mom kidding each other and Pop stealing kisses from her.

Mom worked constantly on her presentations for the convention. On top of her lesson planning and homework, she had additional work for the convention. Mom was very aware that she was delivering an important verdict on the new language arts initiative. Many of the teachers in the room would be older and more experienced than she was. They would be listening very closely to what she had to say. Who was this woman trying to change how they had been teaching for decades?

Many of the teachers would reject everything Mom was saying. Many would reject her as well, and she knew it. So Mom was not in the best of moods either. Pop's grumpy attitude was like pouring gasoline on the fires of anxiousness already burning in her heart.

One day after school, Jaris heard Mom on the phone with her mother. "No," Mom was saying, "he's not home yet. I dread him coming home. He's deliberately staying late at the garage to punish me for going to this convention. He has this childish attitude that a woman's main role in life is wife and mother. To him, everything else is piffle. . . . I know, Mom. I know you did. . . . Yes. . . ." Jaris knew what his grandmother was telling his mother. Her mother was reminding Mom of the times she warned her daughter not to marry Lorenzo Spain.

Chelsea came into Jaris's bedroom. She looked at her brother glumly. "She's on the phone to Grandma Jessie now, complaining about Pop," Chelsea reported glumly.

"Yeah, I know," Jaris replied.

"Now Grandma Jessie will probably want to come over and cause more trouble,"

Chelsea said. "I wish Mom wasn't going to that stupid old convention."

"Yeah, but she has to go," Jaris responded. "It was a big honor for her. If she turned it down, it would be like a slap in the face for the district. The educational publishers got a lot of money invested in these new programs. Mom has to try to make it look good. She really believes in it too. She thinks it'll help the kids learn."

"I hate it that she's going though," Chelsea insisted. "It's not nice around here anymore. Pop's an old grump. Mom's all stressed out and mad at Pop. And another thing too. The other day I saw Elise Maynard. That's Greg Maynard's daughter. She was shopping with her mom. She's coming to Tubman next year. She's in eighth grade at Anderson now. She told me her dad really, *really* likes Mom. She said Mom is his favorite teacher in the whole school!"

Jaris stared at Chelsea. "You mean Maynard's kid told you that?" he gasped.

Greg Maynard had been divorced from his wife for a long time. His children lived with their mother, but they spent many weekends with their father at his luxurious condo.

"Yeah," Chelsea replied. "But I don't like her. Elise is a little sneak. She waited till her mom was at the other end of the store. Then she comes creeping over real catty like. She goes, 'My dad likes your mom a whole bunch.' And I go, 'What's with that? My mom and pop are married, and they're really happy.' And she just giggles. Then her mom comes, and she can't say anything else."

"Kids say stupid things," Jaris asserted. "They don't mean anything."

Chelsea shrugged and left the room. But what she told Jaris made him feel even worse. Mom on the phone with her mother and now this. Jaris's spirits were sinking fast.

# CHAPTER SEVEN

Jaris heard his father's pickup in the driveway. Pop came in, glancing at Mom who was finishing up at the computer. "So, how's it comin, babe," he asked gruffly. "Get that big presentation all done?"

"I'm halfway there, but it's not easy," Mom answered. "A lot of the teachers there aren't going to like this new approach. They want to teach like they've always taught. They tend to resist new approaches."

"Well, if it works, don't fix it, I've always thought," Pop declared. "I think what's screwed up the whole education system is all the time bringing in these new harebrained ideas. Maybe the old crones got the right idea. If it was good enough for us when we went to school, then it's good enough for the kids today. Kids were a lot smarter in the old days. Now they can text and tweet and get on your Facebook and all that stuff. But they don't understand nothin'. My father used to tell me he read *Uncle Tom's Cabin* in grade school. By the time I was in high school, it was too hard for the kids. I remember in my history class, everybody rebelled. Aw nah, we can't read this hard stuff."

Chelsea came into the room. "Our teacher in eighth grade at Anderson, he wanted us to read one chapter of *Uncle Tom's Cabin*. But nobody could even do that. It seemed like a hard adult book."

"I think most of the seniors at Tubman would have problems with it," Jaris agreed, glad that a civil conversation was at least taking place in the house.

But that was soon to end.

"See," Pop asserted, "kids are getting dumber. All the new-fashioned stuff is messing with their minds. Like this language arts garbage you and Maynard been cooking up and cramming down the kids' throats. It's probably all a crock."

"No, actually, it's going to improve learning," Mom replied in an even voice.

"I had to work late tonight," Pop went on, "'cause a lady come in with one of these old Sunbirds. Beautiful car. A ghost from the past. She insisted I do the work. Didn't want the kid getting near the car. This lady really loves that car. She says to me, 'Lorenzo, I wouldn't trust no other mechanic in this whole freakin' town to touch my baby.' That's what she calls the Sunbird. Her baby."

Pop looked around at everyone, as if he expected applause. Then he continued. "I've known her for a couple years. She used to bring in an MG sports car, and I worked on that too. She likes the way I handle your classic-type wheels."

"That's great that your customers trust you, Pop," Jaris said.

"Oh yeah!" Pop cried with a sinister smile. "Quite a car, that Sunbird. Quite a lady too. She comes high steppin' out of that car in these nylon stockings and little silver slippers. She's got legs. I'm tellin' you, they never quit. She looks like some kind of a celebrity. She's one hot chick."

Slowly it dawned on Chelsea and Jaris—and finally Mom. The conversation had nothing whatsoever to do with Pop's mechanical skills. He had a strange grin on his face. Jaris thought a jaguar might be wearing a grin like that as he closed in on his prey. Pop didn't look like Pop at all. He looked almost evil. His voice continued. "Her name is Consuela. Quite a mouthful, eh? Consuela."

Mom had stopped looking at her computer screen. Her head was bowed, and her hands were in her lap.

"So I work on the bird," Pop chatters on, "and get her purrin' like a kitty in about an hour. Consuela, she's so grateful she wants to give me a hug. 'Hey,' I say to myself, 'ain't every day a grease monkey like me gets a chance to hug a lady named Consuela.' So I say, 'Why not?' and she hugs me." Pop chuckled then. Jaris thought the chuckle sounded like a jaguar smacking his lips after devouring the prey.

"So, anyway," Pop rambles on, "Consuela, she's been married a couple, maybe three times. She's got a lot of nice things. The exes come across with lotta money. She's a good kid. I think she musta picked some bad dudes. I look at this hot babe, and I'm thinkin' what kinda fool would let her get away? Anyway, she's comin' back. Turns out she's got a stable of these beautiful old classic cars, and she wants her Lorenzo to work on every one. Yeah, looks like I'll be seeing a lot of her."

Someone must have hit the mute button on the Spain household. It was perfectly quiet for a second or two.

"Well," Pop announced, "gotta shower now, even though I don't smell so bad. Ever notice what happens when you hug somebody wearing really great perfume? The scent sorta clings to you and makes you smell good too?"

Pop strolled down the hall to the bathroom. When the water was running, Mom looked at Jaris and Chelsea.

"You see what he's trying to do, don't you?" Mom hissed in an angry voice.

"What?" Chelsea asked innocently. "Pop is like proud of how much his customers respect him. I mean they let him work on these fabulous old cars."

"Yeah," Jaris agreed. "He's the best mechanic around, that's for sure. You gotta be good not to mess up an old classic."

"Don't play dumb, you guys," Mom commanded bitterly. "He's trying to make me jealous. He's furious that I'm going to New Orleans to that convention and that Greg is going too. He wants me to think some trashy woman is bringing in her ritzy cars and fawning over him!"

Chelsea and Jaris looked at one another. Of course they knew that too. It was Pop's new strategy. Two can play the game. When the cat's away, the mouse will play.

"This man is so infantile," Mom declared. "He's comparing my difficult educational challenge with him supposedly fooling around with a floozy."

Pop emerged from the shower, dried off and dressed in a new T-shirt and jeans. He looked very good. "For a guy my age, I'm in pretty good shape, eh babe?" he remarked.

"Yes, Lorenzo," Mom agreed. "You're a real macho man. I'm surprised that *GQ* magazine hasn't contacted you yet."

"Hey, give 'em time," Pop insisted. "You know, there's a fitness center around the corner from my garage. I pop in there sometimes to work on the old abs. I work out, check my weight. It's all good. I'm six foot two, one seventy pounds. Lean and mean. Just about perfect. Real good BMI, that there is—"

"Body mass index," Mom snapped. "I know a few things."

"Yeah, well," Pop went on, "I'm a twenty-one on the BMI. The cute little chick who works in the fitness place is real impressed with that. All the chicks in the spa, real lookers. Young, but they know their stuff. I got hard abs. But as I get older, maybe I need to hang out there more. I can do it now with Darnell doin' so good. Make sure I keep healthy and fit. And the chicks in there, real easy on the eyes, if you get my meaning," Pop said, once again smiling like a jaguar.

"Are you about done, Lorenzo?" Mom snapped. "Because I'm trying to concentrate. I have serious work to do."

"Sure babe!" Pop replied. "Heaven forbid I should interrupt the newest scheme to screw up kids' minds. Those poor little devils trapped in school with the so-called educators messing with their heads. So just ignore me, Monie. Right now I'm talkin' to Jaris and Chelsea."

Pop dramatically turned to the kids. "See, you guys," he told them, "your mom and Maynard, they want to give the schools another spin. They want to turn them more upside down than they are already. Few of the poor kids caught on to reading and writing a little better. We can't let that happen. Gotta dumb them down some." Pop's grin widened. "And speaking of Greg Maynard, now there's a dude who needs to go to the fitness center more often. Needs to lose some of that flab. This is a guy who's lettin' himself go a little too much. I don't know what a short guy like him oughta weigh. But he's like five foot five inches, somethin' like that. Why, he probably tips the scale at a couple hundred would you say?"

Mom looked outraged.

Chelsea quickly covered her mouth to hide her giggling. She thought Greg Maynard was more like five eleven, but it wasn't important. He wasn't fat, but he didn't look really good like Pop either.

"Hey babe," Pop said to Mom, "you and that Maynard dude'll be riding in the riverboats on the Mississippi. When you do, mention to him about the fitness center. Tell him they're good at getting' rid of those rubber tires." Pop chuckled then and went outside.

Jaris didn't think things could get any worse. Then he heard a car in the driveway. For a moment, he thought Grandma Jessie had decided to launch a sneak attack on the family. But what happened was even worse than a visit from Grandma Jessie. Greg Maynard was parking his miniature, environmentally friendly car alongside Pop's truck. Pop was outside admiring his newly planted fall vegetables in the twilight. So he was the first to see Mom's principal.

"Oh, good evening Mr. Spain," Greg Maynard greeted. "My, you must be so proud of your wife being chosen to attend our big convention in New Orleans. That indeed is quite an honor."

"Hey lissen," Pop responded, "I'd be real proud if she won that Nobel Peace Prize they give out over there in Oslo. You know the one I mean—for people who change the course of history for all humanity. Or if she won one of those Pulitzer Prizes for writing the novel of the century. But hey, gettin' a chance to go to New Orleans and hang around with a bunch of batty old teachers? Or arguing about how to mess up public education even more than it is already? Man, that has got to be the thrill of a lifetime."

Mom was at the computer when she heard the familiar voice of Greg Maynard and then Pop's voice. A look of horror gripped her face. She almost fell over her chair to reach the door.

"Ahhh," Mr. Maynard replied, unsure of how to react to Pop's astonishing tirade. "Well . . ."

"Hey!" Pop crowed, circling Mr. Maynard's little car. "Look at this little machine you come in. Is that a real car? Or did you borrow one of those bumper cars the kids ride in at the fair?"

"N-no," Mr. Maynard stammered. "It's a very good new car with excellent gas mileage. Gets double the gas mileage of most cars."

"Hey, I bet it does," Pop agreed. "Little car like that, you move it along with your legs? Seems like you could just put your feet down on the street and stop it. You know, like the kids do."

Mom was trying to wrench the front door open, but she'd forgotten to unlock it in her nervousness.

"Well," Mr. Maynard suggested, "I better go inside and see . . . your wife . . . and give her this . . . uh . . . material we've printed for the convention. She . . . uh . . . needs it for her, you know, presentation." Mr. Maynard was babbling now. As he grasped the door, Mom swung it open. They almost fell into each other. Jaris was standing alongside Mom. Mr. Maynard gave him a sick smile. Then he turned to Monica Spain, whose expression showed total mortification.

"Hi," Mom gasped. "Oh, you brought the stuff we talked about. That's . . . good . . ."

"Yes, here it is," Mr. Maynard burbled. He kept glancing behind him. He seemed worried that Pop might come in and join the conversation. "So, are we about ready for the big day, Monica?"

"Yes, I have everything done . . . just about," Mom answered. Meanwhile, she watched in horror as the front door opened, and Pop stuck his head in.

"Hey, Mr. Maynard," Pop interrupted, "I'm keepin' an eye on the kiddie car. Some middle schoolers are out skateboarding this evening. We don't want them carrying it off for their younger brothers and sisters, you know." Pop's head disappeared behind the door.

Mom and Greg Maynard exchanged looks. Then Mr. Maynard looked at his wrist watch. "Well, better be off," he mumbled, escaping outside. He jumped in his car.

As he was backing from the driveway, Mom glared at Jaris and Chelsea. "Did your father insult Mr. Maynard out there? Did you hear anything?" she demanded.

"No, Mom," Jaris answered solemnly. "He was just telling Mr. Maynard what a nice little car he had."

"Yes," Chelsea pitched in loyally. "He was saying how cute it was. Mom, did you *see* Mr. Maynard's car? I had one almost as big when I was four years old. Only it was pink."

"Chelsea!" Mom snarled. "Your push-pull toy was *not* almost as big as Greg's car."

Pop came in then. "Well, he's gone," he announced. "That little car goes real fast. Reminded me of a toy rocket."

"Lorenzo," Mom demanded, "did you insult my principal?" She felt she could no longer rely on what her children told her. They were blindly loyal to their father. Lorenzo Spain could dump fertilizer on Mr. Maynard's head, but they would just call it a gift.

"Hey babe," Pop whined in a hurt voice, "what kind of a guy do you think I am? I didn't insult the little fat guy. I didn't even tell him about the fitness center. I could have said how much he needed to take care of that weight problem he's got. But I didn't."

Mom glared at him. "Well," Pop continued, "he asked me if I was proud of you for being picked to go to that convention. I told him I was as proud as if you'd won the Nobel Peace Prize or maybe that Pulitzer Prize. Yeah, I was nice, babe. I was on my best behavior, y'hear what I'm sayin'?"

Mom stared at Pop, not knowing what to believe. She suspected he had been so sarcastic that Mr. Maynard got the message.

"And then we got to talkin' about cars, like guys do, you know," Pop continued. "Course Maynard, he ain't much of a man's man. But what else can we talk about? Kiddie lit? I figure we coulda talked about football. But, I'm thinking, this guy wouldn't know a quarterback from a humpbacked whale. Only game he'd know about would be tiddlywinks."

Mom was still speechless, and Pop rattled on "So I was tellin' him how nice it was that he got one of those little bumper cars from the fair. He kinda makes it go with his legs. Hey, that's good! 'Cause he's saving gas and protecting the environment. I gotta hand it to the man for that. He's goin' green in a big way. How many grown men would pedal around town in a kiddie car just to help the animals and the trees?"

"I'm going to bed," Mom announced grimly.

Pop looked at Jaris and Chelsea and winked. "She thinks I ain't comin'" he whispered. "She thinks I ain't got the nerve, but here I go."

As Pops strutted down the hall, Jaris and Chelsea retreated to their rooms. Jaris's bedroom was right next to his parents' room. He heard their voices through the wall.

"I shudder to think what Greg Maynard is making of you, Lorenzo," Mom was saying. "He must think he stopped off at a mad house."

"Hey babe," Pop replied, "what can I say? I don't like him much either."

Mom's voice was pained. "I can't believe you won't show him a little goodwill and respect just because he *is* my principal."

"Hey," Pop insisted, "he comes drivin' up here in that little bumper car. I was sprinkling my peppers and broccoli plants when it's nearly dark. You know, like the water cops tell us we have to do when it don't rain enough. So anyway, when I see him, I got this big urge to turn the hose on him. I wanted to get him right in the kisser with the spray. I wanted to do that, but I didn't Monie. I restrained myself from doin' that. Y'hear what I'm sayin'? Now if that ain't respect, I don't know what is."

The voices stopped then. Jaris stared at the illuminated face of his clock. It was almost ten thirty. He breathed a sigh of relief. The day had ended without something even worse happening.

Then the dark thoughts started to flood Jaris's mind. Tomorrow, he had a progress report in AP American History, as well as tests in math and English. Even lunch was probably going to be hard. Maybe Carissa would show up under the eucalyptus trees trying to make up with Kevin. Of course, that wouldn't work. Then she would make everybody feel bad and start crying again. Nobody's lunch would taste good with her bawling. Then maybe Marko Lane would try to humiliate Lydell Nelson again. This time, Kevin Walker would tear Marko's ears off his head. All these miserable possibilities swirled in Jaris's brain. He just couldn't get to sleep for the rest he needed.

But then Jaris remembered what Sereeta said Ms. McDowell had told her. "Don't think about tomorrow." So Jaris turned over, closed his eyes, and pushed all those thoughts out of his mind.

# CHAPTER EIGHT

The next day, Jaris was heading for lunch. He hoped Carissa wouldn't be hanging around moping. As he neared the spot under the eucalyptus trees, he saw all his old friends. Trevor Jenkins was coming down the trail and Jaris grabbed his hand. "Hey, what's hap'nin, bro?"

Trevor grinned. "I got the courage to ask Shay in speech class to go for frozen yogurt after school. She said okay!"

"Way to go, man," Jaris said.

They all settled down and started eating.

Sereeta glanced over at Jaris. He was munching a ham and cheese sandwich Pop made for him. Pop was now routinely making lunches for Jaris and Chelsea. They were wonderful. You never knew what was coming next—celery sticks, broccoli, salsa, pickle relish, hot sauce. "How's it going for you, babe?" Sereeta asked.

"Mom's busy getting ready for the convention," Jaris said, still chewing a bite of sandwich. "Pop is gonna miss her. I dread those four days."

"Tonight I cook dinner for Mom and Perry," Sereeta announced. "I cooked that apricot glazed pork with rice for me and Grandma last night. It turned out good. I'm gonna make that. Grandma said it was delicious. Course, Grandma is so nice she might not always tell the truth. So I told her it was really important that she's gotta be honest. Then she fessed up and said something was missing. Turned out the hoisin sauce was missing."

Oliver laughed. "What's hoisin sauce?" he asked.

"It's like oyster sauce, I guess," Sereeta replied. "I didn't have any, so I'm using oyster sauce. It's a real easy recipe. You just stir-fry the pork and add broccoli, cauliflower and carrots. Then the apricot and oyster sauce, and stir it up. You serve it with rice. I don't think I can screw it up."

"It sounds scrumptious," Alonee said. "I wish I was coming to dinner."

"I wish you were coming too," Sereeta said. "I wish I was cooking for Mom and Jaris, and all you guys. Anybody but Perry Manley. But I can't feel that way. The whole purpose of this is to make us one happy family." Sereeta grimaced. "I gotta try really, really hard to be nice to Perry. You never know when you've got him miffed. I call Mom every night now, and she seems good. But I don't know."

After a moment of silence, Oliver looked at Jaris. "I went to the fitness center the other day," Oliver said, "and I saw your dad. Man, that guy looks really good. He was lifting a few weights. He was doing better than guys half his age."

"He's worked hard all his life," Jaris explained, "lifting auto parts, dragging tires around. Lifting barbells is easy. I've never seen Pop with an extra ounce of fat on him."

"My dad has to lose some weight," Alonee remarked. "Firemen can't put on excess pounds."

Derrick grinned. "My poor pa is having trouble getting up the ladder to fix roofs. Mom yells at him all the time. 'Guthrie, don't you dare take another piece of that fried chicken!'" Derrick said.

"Hey Jaris," Oliver said, "your Pop's getting the eye from some of the chicks in that fitness center. He'd pass for a dude in his thirties."

Sami and Matson arrived then. They heard what Oliver was saying. Sami advised, "Jaris, your mama better rein that dude in. He oughtn't to be at the fitness center showing off that hard body." Sami was just joking. She didn't realize that she had hit a raw nerve with Jaris.

Sami's kidding comment started up all those dark thoughts in Jaris's mind. Pop was really steamed about Mom going to New Orleans because Greg Maynard was part of the group. His reaction was unreasonable, but he *was* steamed. Things wouldn't be so bad if Greg Maynard wasn't going too. They wouldn't be so bad if Maynard hadn't always made it clear that he really liked Mom. Or if Maynard wasn't divorced and lonely, living all by himself in his condo. Or if Maynard wasn't always sitting in the Spain living room. Or if he didn't seem so educated and charming when Pop was at his worst. When Pop drank a little too much, he'd roar around the house venting his dark thoughts.

Jaris tried to stop thinking such wild thoughts. His parents loved each other. They had always argued, sometimes heatedly. But they always made up and seemed to love each other even more. Surely they would keep on loving each other no matter what. The bonds were too strong for either of them ever to break them.

But Jaris couldn't know what was going through his father's mind. Nobody knows what another person is thinking. Pop didn't like the fact that Mom was more educated than he was. Sometimes he felt inferior to her, even if he was the owner of a successful garage. It rankled him that his wife was a professional going off to a convention in New Orleans while he was repairing beaters. True, it was *his* garage. But he was still a grease monkey, and the cars were still beaters.

Jaris imagined some pretty twenty-four–year-old at the gym smiling at his dad. What would go through Pop's mind? "Wow! She think's I'm hot." Jaris shuddered and pushed the fears from his mind. He told himself that, before he knew it, Mom would be gone and back from New Orleans. Everything would be normal again.

"Sereeta," Jaris spoke up suddenly. "Let's go to a concert tomorrow night in the park. Some guys playing the blues. I know it's not the loud banging music you like, babe. But I'd just like you to hear these guys. I'm really getting into the blues. I'm listening to Pop's old music, and it's really cool. I put some old vinyl music on my iPod, by a guy named Blind Lemon Jefferson. I never heard of him until a few weeks ago. But he's got this really lonesome, painful sound that gets to me."

"Sure Jaris, I'd love to go," Sereeta agreed.

For the rest of the lunch break, Jaris focused on his date with Sereeta for tomorrow night. He tried to forget Greg Maynard and the chicks noticing Pop at the gym. He just kept thinking of being with Sereeta. And he looked forward to listening to the music he was growing to love.

After lunch, Langston Myers arrived in class in high good humor. Jaris had never seen him so happy.

"Before we begin class this afternoon," Mr. Myers announced, "I have very exciting news. The novel I have been working on for several years is in the hands of my editor, and it shall be published soon. It is set during the heady days of the Harlem Renaissance, and I'm quite confident it will be very successful. We might even be seeing it on the best-seller lists."

Some of the students in the room applauded. No student in the room honestly cared whether Mr. Myers became a published author. But applauding seemed the polite, and prudent, thing to do. After all, he'd been working on the novel for a long time, and getting it published was an achievement. Jaris had vague dreams of someday writing something himself and seeing it published. He could imagine how excited and happy he would be if that ever happened.

Jaris thought for a moment. What must it feel like to hold a book in your hand and see your own name on the spine? He couldn't blame Mr. Myers for being ecstatic. The English quiz consisted of some quotes the class had read and discussed. Jaris thought it was easy. He recognized all the authors, and he filled in their names. He followed instructions and chose one of the quotes to write a short essay on. Jaris was finished before the time for the test was over. But when he glanced over at Marko, he could see he was having trouble.

"Uh Mr. Myers," Marko said, raising his hand, "I'll have to take a makeup on this. My brain injury is kicking in again. I am all confused, sir."

Mr. Myers did not like Marko Lane. He had gone out of his way to allow Marko to do a lot of work in English while recuperating from his injury at home. But Mr. Myers had been assured that Marko was now fine and that he could be treated as any other student. Marko should be able to take tests just like everybody else. Mr. Myers strongly suspected that Marko had just not studied for the test. Now he was using his physical condition as an excuse.

"I'm sorry, Mr. Lane," Mr. Myers replied crisply. "If you felt ill at the beginning of the test, you should have come up here to explain. It is unacceptable to bow out almost at the end."

"You don't understand, Mr. Myers," Marko insisted. "It like comes on all of a sudden. I get this spacey feeling, and I'm not sure where I am."

Several students snickered.

"Mr. Lane, please see your physician," Mr. Myers suggested. "Have him write a letter explaining these strange spells you are subject to. I shall reconsider. Otherwise, this test stands as it is." Mr. Myers seemed extremely annoyed.

As the class filed out, Jaris was still at his desk, double-checking his report for AP American History. It was due today.

Jaris overheard Marko talking to Jasmine. "The old fool wouldn't buy it, babe. I forgot all about us having this stupid test today. You were with me at the club last night, Jasmine, why didn't you remind me we had a test today and we needed to study?"

"I gotta remind you of everything, boy?" Jasmine snapped back. "How come nothin' is ever your own fault, Marko. It's always somebody else's fault. You're a big boy, fool. I went home way before you did last night. I remember sayin', 'Dude, school tomorrow. I can't party all night.' But you just smiled and waved at me. I hadda hitch a ride with my cousins 'cause you havin' too much fun to get home!"

"This test grade is gonna bring me down bad, girl," Marko whined. "Myers is such an idiot. The test didn't even make sense. All those stupid quotes. Who cares what those crazy old dudes said hundreds of years ago? Myers is a lousy teacher. All he cares about is his stupid book."

Jaris shook his head and smiled to himself. Alonee and Oliver were walking beside him.

"Poor Marko," Alonee commented. "He can't ever stop being Marko."

Lydell came along, looking for Kevin. When he saw him, he cried, "Kev, I really aced that test. I think I got an A!"

Kevin flashed a nice grin. It was good to see Kevin smiling. He had been looking pretty glum since he and Carissa split. "Way to go, dude!" he told Lydell.

"I think goin' to the gym is helping my brains," Lydell remarked. "Making the blood flow." He still clutched his journal tightly under his arm. He wasn't going to let Marko sneak up behind him and rip out a page again.

Marko didn't like Jaris Spain, but they were about the same in intelligence. Both boys had better-than-average IQs, but neither was near the brilliance of Oliver Randall. The major difference between Jaris and Marko was that Jaris studied hard. He knew he wasn't a genius; so he became an overachiever. Marko liked playing too much to spend unending hours studying, as Jaris did. So Marko usually ended up with a grade lower than Jaris.

"Hey Spain, wasn't that a lousy test?" he asked. "I think the tests this guy gives are even stupider than what we used to get from old Pippin."

"No, actually it was pretty straightforward," Jaris objected. "He talked about this stuff a lot, and I studied for about an hour last night. Chelsea quizzed me on the names of the guys making those quotes so that I wouldn't get them mixed up. Did you study much, Marko?"

"Yeah, I studied hard," Marko lied.

Jasmine poked Marko in the ribs. "Liar!" she accused him. "You didn't study at all, sucka. You dropped me off and then met your friends. You didn't get home till late."

All the time Jasmine was talking, Marko was paying no attention. He was glaring at Langston Myers as the teacher strode from the classroom.

Just then, Mr. Pippin came to the door with his poor, miserable, battered briefcase. He was still carrying it after many, many years.

"Hello Mr. Pippin," Mr. Myers cried in an exuberant voice. "My book is going to be published finally, old boy!"

"Congratulations!" Mr. Pippin responded. "That is a truly marvelous accomplishment. I think all of us English teachers have that dream—that one day we will be published. I know I did many years ago, but the publishers kept turning me down. Finally I packed my dear old manuscript away where it still is, turning yellow. What is your book about?"

"Ah, it's quite a juicy drama," Mr. Myers replied buoyantly, "with overtones of mystery. The story is set in Harlem during the Renaissance there in the twenties. It's a honey of a book, my man. It is filled with colorful characters as well as real people who lived during that time, people like Josephine Baker and Bessie Smith."

"Wonderful!" Mr. Pippin said, trying to be enthusiastic about another man's success. Nothing grand like this had ever happened to Mr. Pippin. Mr. Myers was younger than Mr. Pippin by some twenty years. Mr. Pippin had buried all his dreams, one by one. Now, in his final teaching years, he couldn't even control the discipline in his own classroom, whereas Mr. Myers had good order in his. Mr. Myers even succeeded in cowing that monster, Marko Lane, who had tormented Mr. Pippin. And now—the final indignity for Mr. Pippin—Mr. Myers was a published author.

Mr. Myers worked his way down the hall, repeating the good news to other teachers.

Marko Lane watched him from a distance, full of rage. How could that pompous fool have a book published, Marko thought? Marko had heard that Myers had shopped the book around for a long time without success. Getting a book published was hard. And all Myers had ever published were ridiculous poems in journals like *Mississippi Mud Ink*. He was paid for his work only in free copies. Now a publisher was buying his book? How could it be, Marko wondered?

"I think he's lyin'," Marko said to Jasmine.

"What do you care, sucka?" she snapped. "It got nothin' to do with you. If some boring old teacher got his dumb book published, it ain't nothin' to you or me." She was still in a bad mood from last night when Marko was ogling that long-legged singer.

"I'm goin' to look on the Internet and see who's publishing his book," Marko declared darkly. "If he's got a book comin' out, it oughta be there."

"You can't be happy unless you're goring somebody, can you, boy?" Jasmine sneered. "I don't know why I stick with you. You like a mean old bull elephant stompin' on everybody, looking for somebody to be mad at."

"I told that old fool Myers," Marko fumed, "that I got sick during the test. He wouldn't have no sympathy for me. I almost got killed when that guy hit me with the baseball bat. Myers ought to have sympathy for somebody almost got killed. He won't let me take a makeup test unless I get a letter from my doctor sayin' I get these spacey spells."

"So go to your doctor and get his letter," Jasmine told him.

"That old quack is gonna say I'm fine. He won't back me up," Marko insisted.

"Then take your medicine like a man, Marko," Jasmine advised. "You blew the test 'cause you didn't study. It's your bad."

"I'm gonna search the Internet," Marko snarled. "I'm gonna see if I can't trip that old Myers up."

Jaris had overheard it all. Marko couldn't help being Marko. Jaris finished checking his report and left the room.

At school the next day, Jaris was waiting for Sereeta at Harriet Tubman's statue. Jaris wanted to know how last night went. He had thought about calling her last night and finding out. But she wouldn't be home before ten. He didn't want to bother her much later just to satisfy his own curiosity. He figured if it had gone badly and she needed support, she would have called him. But Sereeta was smiling this morning, reassuring Jaris that the night went well.

"It was good, babe," she reported, kissing Jaris on the cheek. "Perry was almost nice. And the baby was there in his high chair, poor little Jake, looking around with his big eyes. He actually smiled at me. It gave me goose bumps."

Sereeta crouched a little and wiggled her head. Her eyes widened, and she clutched her books in front of her. "*My little brother!* Is that wild or what?" She laughed gently. "I look at Jake and I freak out, Jaris. He looks so cute. I dragged out my old baby pictures the other day. I looked at myself when I was his age, and I could see a resemblance. Mom says the same thing, but not when Perry is around. Oh Jaris, remember how awful I was when

Mom was expecting Jake? I thought he was replacing me in Mom's life, taking all the love that I deserved away from me. I wanted him to be a mean, bratty baby just to get even. I was such a monster, Jaris."

"You were just sad and lonely about losing your mom," Jaris consoled. "You're a good, kind person. But you were scared you were getting written out of the picture. You didn't mean the stuff you said."

"You're such an angel, Jaris. I don't deserve you," Sereeta sighed. "I'm not as nice as you, Jaris. But then nobody is. So I don't feel so bad . . ."

"I'm not that good," Jaris objected. "Come on. I have my dark side."

"Jaris, the thing is," Sereeta said in a shaky voice. "The thing is . . . I think I love him. Jake. I think I love my little brother. I get this weird feeling now when I see him. He looks so precious to me, his chubby little arms, his little fists."

"That's great, Sereeta," Jaris told her. "There's nothing bad about that. What's that old song say? 'What the world needs now is love sweet love.' The more people you love, the happier you are."

"I'm stupid happy right now," Sereeta said. "Grandma packed me a nice lunch, we got no tests today, and tonight we get to be together. It doesn't get any better than that."

Jaris was starting to talk about the music they would hear tonight when Marko Lane sprinted by as if running the race of his life. "Uh-oh, what's that now?" Jaris groaned.

Marko caught up to Jasmine. He was talking so loud that anyone on the campus could hear him. "Babe," Marko was yelling. "I got the scoop! You won't believe it, Jaz. It's just sweet! It's so sweet!"

"What're you talkin' about, boy?" Jasmine responded in an annoyed voice. "Everybody looking at us. Give it up, tell me what's hap'nin. You win the lottery or something?"

"It's not a real publisher," Marko crowed. "They got old Myers's book for sale on the Internet, but it's put out by what they call a subsidy press. That means he paid to have the book published. A regular publisher gives you an advance, and then you get royalties from the books that sell. But this is different. You pay them a big chunk of money, and they print whatever garbage you've written. Anybody can get published like this. They print the books and send them to you. Then you gotta sell them yourself. Old Myers has nothing to brag about. He paid for his stupid piece of trash to be published."

"How'd you find that out?" Jasmine asked.

"I got to old Myers' Web site," Marko started to explain. "He's selling the books from there. He's tellin' the big news right there. He got the name of the publisher and I never heard of them. So I check it out, and it's one of these subsidy deals. I mean, some old lady could write a book on how to raise petunias, and they'd put that out if she had the money. It's no big honor like Myers was trying to make out. It's a crock,

Jasmine. Man, that old fool isn't goin' to be ridin' so high when this gets around."

"Oh brother!" Jaris moaned to Sereeta. "Did you get that?"

"Yeah," Sereeta replied sadly, "that's going to be so humiliating to Mr. Myers. There he is, telling everybody the big news about his novel getting published. Everybody just figured it was a regular book deal, and now . . ."

Jaris and Sereeta hurried over to where Marko was holding forth. Now a dozen students were listening.

"Hey Marko," Jaris asked, "you sure you want to be doing this? Mr. Myers maybe did write a good book, but the book business is pretty tight now. Maybe this was the only way to get it out right now. Sometimes really good books get published by subsidy presses. Then they do well, and regular publishers pick them up. That's happened lots of times."

"Yeah, right," Marko sneered, gloating over his discovery.

"Dude, he's not gonna like you very much when he finds out what you're doing," Jaris advised.

"He hates me anyway," Marko said. "Remember when that lunatic Kevin Walker attacked me just 'cause I took a page from wacko Lydell's journal? Old Myers came along and blamed me. I way lying there on the ground where Walker had hurled me, and I got blamed for the thing. I was just trying to find out what crazy ideas that wacko Lydell had, and I get to be the bad guy. Now it's payback time. Let's see how old Myers likes it when the truth comes out."

Mr. Pippin came along on his way to junior English. When he saw Marko Lane, he tried to change direction. But Marko leaped into his path. "Mr. Myers is a fraud, Mr. Pippin!" Marko crowed. "He didn't sell no book to a publisher. He paid to have it published himself!" For a moment it looked like Mr. Pippin was going to hit Marko with his old, battered briefcase.

Jaris stepped back. If Mr. Pippin did hit Marko with the old briefcase, it seemed like it would explode. They'd be showered with all the papers, pens, and whatever other items Mr. Pippin had been collecting for the past thirty years.

"You hear what I'm sayin' Mr. Pippin?" Marko insisted. "Old Myers did not sell his book to nobody. He's paying to have it published. Don't you get it? He's a liar and a fraud.

"I don't have to put up with you anymore, Marko Lane," Mr. Pippin almost sobbed. "Go away!" Mr. Pippin looked imploringly at Jaris. "Jaris, please, get Ms. McDowell to make him go away."

As Jaris made a move toward Ms. Torie McDowell's classroom, Marko split. Jaris figured Mr. Pippin didn't need Ms. McDowell anymore.

# CHAPTER NINE

Later that day, Kevin Walker and Lydell Nelson walked together to one of their classes. Lydell had made a few notes in his journal. Then he stuck the page back into his binder.

"You ever let anybody read your journal, Lydell?" Kevin asked in a matter-of-fact voice.

"Oh no," Lydell replied. "I'd be ashamed."

"Like nobody in your family even read it?" Kevin asked.

"Especially not them," Lydell insisted. "My aunt thinks I'm crazy anyway. She's always saying I got no friends and I'm weird. Her kids, my cousins, they laugh at me all the time. I'd die of embarrassment if anybody read my journal. That's why I got so upset when Marko Lane ripped out a page. I sure am grateful you got it back for me."

"How long you been writing in there, Lydell?" Kevin inquired.

"Since he died," Lydell said. "It was to him at first. I couldn't talk to him anymore, so I wrote to him. I wrote down what I was feeling, and it was sorta a way to tell him."

"Your pa, huh?" Kevin said.

"Yeah," Lydell answered. "We used to talk and talk. He was a big talker. But then . . ."

"Lydell, if you ever want me to read some of it, I'd be glad to," Kevin offered. "I swear to you I wouldn't laugh or anything."

Lydell looked at his new friend. Kevin was maybe the only friend he'd had in his life, excluding his father, who was his best friend. "You'd think I was nuts like everybody else does if you read my journal," Lydell objected.

"I'm nuts too, Lydell," Kevin assured him. "So I don't believe folks who live in glass houses should throw stones. You get my meaning? Look, I'm no expert on good writing. I'm hanging on in English because I study a lot. But I've read a lotta books, mostly paperback mysteries. I like that kind of stuff. I couldn't tell you what good writing is, but I know what keeps my interest. I won't make bad comments about your journal, Lydell."

Lydell fell silent. He had not shown his journal to a living soul in all the years since he began writing it. He never felt safe enough with anybody to share something so personal. It was like ripping a veil off his soul and standing there with all his thoughts exposed to the naked light. But deep in his heart he always wanted somebody to read his journal. He never knew who it would be, but he wanted to share it.

And Lydell trusted Kevin more than he had trusted anybody since his father was alive.

"Okay," Lydell agreed. "You can read my journal. But you got to promise me you won't tell anybody what's in there."

"Man, I'll protect it with my life," Kevin pledged. He grinned at Lydell. "I'll put it in my backpack, Lydell, and I won't even tell anybody I'm reading it. Okay?"

"Okay, Kevin," Lydell replied, handing him the journal.

Kevin hadn't been eating his lunch under the eucalyptus trees with his friends lately. He knew that Carissa was hanging there. He didn't want to see her or talk to her or listen to her lame excuses. So Kevin found a remote spot on campus near where the track team practiced. He sat on a patch of grass and took his hot dog sandwich out of the bag. He pulled out Lydell's journal and began to read it.

The journal told the story of life at the Nelson house where Lydell had lived since his father's death.

Lydell wrote:

The tantalizing aroma of apple pie came from the house when I got home. Aunt Laney makes good pies. I thought about the pie all the time I was changing from my school clothes to my grungy clothes. Most of the time we'd have rice pudding for dessert. It was only big heaps of half-cooked rice and hard little raisins that looked and tasted like pebbles. I hated the rice pudding because there was never enough sugar in it.

But today was going to be special. My mouth was all ready for the apple pie. Me and my father used to go to a little café in town. We'd have a slice of apple pie and coffee on Sunday. Often my pa would pay a little extra, and there would be a dollop of ice cream on the pie crust. That was always amazing.

I wondered if there might be ice cream on the apple pie too. And I thought that was too much to hope for. But I kept it as a secret hope.

My cousins smelled the apple pie too. When dinner was finished, Aunt Laney brought it, still warm from the oven. Aunt

Laney smiled at her children, but she gave me a hard look. "Don't be getting ideas," she said to me. She told me I was too fat anyway and I didn't need any apple pie. The truth was, Aunt Laney and Uncle Anson had three children of their own. That would mean cutting the apple pie in five pieces. That would mean a good slice for each of them. Cutting it in six pieces would be taking from them to give to me. Aunt Laney didn't want to do that. So I watched her put the hot apple pie slices on the five dishes. Aunt Laney told me there was leftover rice pudding from yesterday if I wanted dessert. Aunt Laney put a dollop of peach ice cream on each of the apple slices. I told her she didn't need to give me any rice pudding.

I tried not to watch them eat.

Kevin kept reading the journal. He couldn't put it down. It was funny in places, sad and scary in other places. It was heartbreaking and terrifying. Lydell talked about how his father died. He talked about having dreams about finding the men who killed his father and doing terrible things to them. That part was raw and ugly.

Kevin was shaken by the journal. It was life at a dark edge where most people never go. But Kevin had been to that place himself, and he understood. There was deep overpowering despair in the journal. There were also bright slivers of hope, sticking out in unexpected places. Some time after Lydell's dad died, an old lady stopped Lydell on the street. He didn't know who she was. But she said she was an old friend of his father. She gave Lydell a hundred dollar bill. She said, "Bless you, my child" and walked on. And the despair lifted, if only for a little while.

Kevin didn't see Lydell again until well after school. Kevin wasn't going to the gym today. He'd promised Coach Curry he'd come to track practice. The meet against arch rival Lincoln was coming up. Marko Lane had been cleared by his doctor to participate, and that made Kevin nauseous. But he'd come anyway and run the best he could. He respected Coach Curry and he loved the team. He wouldn't let Marko's presence mess it up for him. He enjoyed being with Trevor and Matson.

Trevor and Matson were running up to their best levels. Kevin was faster than he had been in a while. Marko lagged, blaming it on his recent injury. Coach Curry had a grouchy look on his face, and he told Marko to practice more.

"Lot of our hopes are riding on you Twister," Coach Curry told Kevin at the end of practice. He clapped Kevin on the shoulder.

During Kevin's trial run for the coach, he'd made his best time ever. But the run reminded him of the first days he ran at Tubman. Carissa Polson would stand on the sidelines and yell "Go Twister!" She'd jump up and down, her braids flying atop her head. Kevin got a kick out of her. He hated to admit it, even to himself, but he missed her terribly.

Kevin remembered when Carissa would fly into his arms after a race, almost knocking him down. Right now he closed his eyes and remembered how soft and warm she felt in his arms. She was a crazy chick, but she meant a lot to him. He shook his head, as if to dislodge her memory.

Kevin showered back in the gym and came outside in his T-shirt and jeans, ready to jog home. The sun was beginning to go down.

"Hi," she called, standing in the late afternoon shadows. She must have been standing there a long time. "Hi, Twister."

Kevin stood there, looking at Carissa. He didn't say anything.

"I watched you run today," Carissa told him. "You were just a blur. I wanted to cheer, but I thought you'd resent it. I knew you didn't want me to be there. But I had to come, 'cause my heart just aches so much . . . Oh, Kevin, I'm *so sorry* that I hurt you. I understand how you feel. I really do. It's all my fault and—"

"Carrie!" Kevin commanded. "C'mere, babe."

Carissa rushed toward him. Kevin pulled her into his arms and hugged her so tightly that she could hardly breathe. Then he pushed her out at arm's length and said, "You still like frozen green pistachio yogurt, girl?"

Carissa nodded vigorously but did not say the word "yes." She was fighting off tears.

"Okay, babe," Kevin said softly to her. "Tell you what. I have something I gotta do right now. I gotta see someone. It's important to him, and I can't let him down. Y'hear?"

She nodded again.

"All right!" he said. "I should be back in about ten or fifteen minutes. Can you wait here?"

Again, she nodded—and sniffed.

"I'll come back, and then we'll go have ourselves some pistachio yogurt," Kevin promised. "And we'll have a long talk, like we always used to."

Kevin left Carissa and looked for Lydell but didn't see him right away. Kevin jogged to the east side of the campus and finally spotted Lydell starting his walk home. Lydell rarely went right home after school. Kevin knew he hung around the library for a while, killing time. Lydell's shoulders were slumping, as usual. And his head was down, as usual. He didn't look very happy about having to go home.

"Hey, Lydell," Kevin shouted. "I got something that belongs to you."

Lydell turned, his eyes wide with tension. Kevin had read his journal. Kevin now knew things about him that nobody else on earth knew. Kevin knew his terrors and his demons—the often pathetic details of his life. Did Kevin now think he was crazy, or a fool, or just a loner? Did reading the journal ruin the friendship that meant so much to Lydell? Lydell was already regretting letting Kevin see it.

"Dude," Kevin said when he got closer. "This is good stuff. I couldn't stop reading.

It's gripping. You got a way with words, man. I even lose interest in my murder mysteries sometimes, and I flip them shut. But I read your stuff straight through, and it got me here." Kevin tapped a couple of fingers over his heart.

Lydell stared at Kevin in amazement and relief. "You don't think it's all just the ravings of a lunatic?" he asked.

"No man. It's good!" Kevin objected. "I think you should let Mr. Myers see it."

Lydell looked shocked. "Oh no, I couldn't show it to him. He's a brilliant, educated man. He's written a novel, and it's gonna be published. He's an important man. I'd never have the courage to show it to him."

"You should, man," Kevin urged him. "It's real. It's powerful, from the heart. Over the years I've had to read a lot of stuff in school. Some of the best books I've read were like memoirs. Y'know, people writing about their own experiences. That's what you've written, and I think Myers would like it."

"Thanks for reading it, Kevin," Lydell said, a smile trembling on his lips. Kevin's compliments had moved him deeply. Lydell could hardly contain the strange new sensations sweeping through him. He didn't know what to make of how he felt. It was almost happiness, something he had not felt in almost eight years.

"No problem, man!" Kevin told him, turning away to get back to Carissa. "Hey! Don't forget what I told you about showing it to Mr. Myers." Kevin took off at a jog. Lydell continued walking home. This time, his head was up, and his shoulders were squared.

In class on Monday afternoon, Langston Myers looked crestfallen. It was all over the campus that his book was self-published. The glow was off his happiness. Jaris felt really sorry for the man. The truth about the book had spread from Marko and his friends to everybody else. Mr. Myers was sure that his colleagues were snickering behind his back or pitying him. He could imagine the wall of whispers. "Poor old Myers," they would be saying. "Nobody would buy his book, so he put it out himself." . . . "Pathetic, eh? Poor guy. Must have been a pretty bad book that it couldn't be sold. I wonder why he bragged about it so much? Didn't he think the truth would come out?"

Lydell sat in his usual place in the last row. He was looking up at the teacher as he discussed the role of parody in literature. Lydell had heard about the teacher publishing his own book because nobody else would buy it. But the stories meant little to Lydell. He knew nothing about the publishing business. To Lydell, a book was a book.

Kevin had urged Lydell to show Mr. Myers his journal. Lydell just couldn't make up his mind. Wouldn't it be wonderful, he thought, if a mature, educated man like Mr. Myers read Lydell's journal and pronounced it worth reading? What if Mr. Myers looked at Lydell's journal and actually found merit in it? Lydell would not have even imagined such a thing possible if Kevin had not been so complimentary.

Surely, Lydell thought, Kevin was just being kind. Nothing so great as a teacher's approval of his journal could ever happen to Lydell. Nothing good happened in Lydell's life for a long time. How could he expect something better than good—something marvelous?

When his father died, all the luck seemed to drain out of Lydell's life. Still, Lydell was tantalized by the slim chance that Kevin was right. Maybe the journal was decent, and Mr. Myers would find it interesting.

Finally, Mr. Myers finished his lecture, and the class began filing out. Lydell pulled his journal from the binder. In this part of the journal were Lydell's most painful feelings. He spoke about his father's death, about witnessing it, about his intense desire to die and go to wherever his beloved father had gone. Here were his vengeful thoughts. Kevin found it all touching and powerful.

Lydell's hand was shaking as he held the journal. He glanced at the teacher who looked older and more weary than usual. He had looked so happy yesterday. Approaching him would have been easier yesterday. The embarrassing flap over his self-published book had taken its toll. He had been buoyant and happy. Now he looked crushed. Lydell thought, "How dare I bother the poor man with my stupid journal? He looks so defeated right now." Lydell even imagined Mr. Myers flying into a rage and screaming at Lydell. "Idiot! Why are you thrusting that immature trash at me? What makes you think some teenage babbling holds any fascination for me?"

Mr. Myers noticed the classroom was empty except for Lydell. He glanced at the boy and asked, "Is there something I can do for you?" It was all the encouragement that Lydell needed.

Lydell almost fell on his face hurrying to the teacher's desk. "Mr. Myers," Lydell stammered, "I keep a journal . . ."

"Oh? That's very good," Mr. Myers replied. "I kept one myself when I was a boy. It's an excellent way of developing one's writing skills." Mr. Myers was speaking in a profoundly disinterested voice.

"I got several of them," Lydell persisted.

"Hmmm," Mr. Myers hummed as he put away the last of his lecture notes in his briefcase. He glanced at his watch. He had no desire to be bantering with a student. He needed to be somewhere else.

"My friend, Kevin Walker, he read one of my journals," Lydell explained. "He said maybe you'd be interested in just looking at it sometime if you didn't have anything else to do."

"Me? What for?" Mr. Myers asked, now seeming more annoyed than disinterested.

"Uh . . . he just said you might, you know . . . like to look at it," Lydell was stammering again, holding his journal before him, offering an unwanted gift.

"All right," Mr. Myers acceded, mainly as a way of getting rid of the odd young man. "I'll look at it. I can't guarantee I'll get to it right away. I have a lot of work for my classes. But I'll get to it." He took the journal and stuffed it into his briefcase with the other materials.

"Thank you, Mr. Myers," Lydell said, fleeing the classroom. It was one of the hardest things he'd ever done. He'd handed his precious, personal journal over to a man who obviously didn't want it. He figured Mr. Myers would probably spend five minutes glancing at it before deciding it was junk.

"Our flight leaves early Friday morning," Mom told Pop as Jaris and Chelsea got home from school. "Greg is going to pick me up around five thirty. We'll go directly to the airport."

"Whoa!" Pop insisted. "Hold it right there, babe. That little fat man in his bumper car from the kiddie park? He's not takin' my wife to the airport. We are taking you, lady. Your family is taking you in a nice safe car. Jaris's car."

"Lorenzo, that would be silly," Mom protested. "You and the kids getting out of bed so early tomorrow morning. Greg is going to the airport anyway and—"

"No way," Pop commanded. "End of story." He stood there looking at Jaris and Chelsea. "What about it, you guys? You want us all to take your mom to the airport tomorrow morning for her big time in New Orleans. Or do you want her to ride in a tiny little bumper car. You know, the one the little fat man borrowed from the fair. Can you imagine that little toy car going down the freeway next to the big rigs and stuff. What do you say?"

"Yeah, Mom," Jaris agreed. "I'd like to go."

Chelsea nodded vigorously. "I want to see you off, Mom," she said. "I don't mind getting up early."

Pop smiled. "See? It's all settled. We all go down there as a family, babe. Lissen up. Who knows what might happen in four days? I could be working at the garage, and the lift could let go and crush me to death. One of the beaters could run wild and run me over. It's very important that we have this nice good-bye at the airport. We might never see each other again on this earth. Y'hear what I'm sayin'?" Pop stood there with his hands swung out from his hips, palms up. A smile danced on his lips. No one could lay it on like Pop could.

"Oh Lorenzo," Mom groaned, "don't say that."

"Hey!" Pop declared. "We walk out the door in the morning, we don't know what's gonna happen that day. Who knows what's gonna happen? We need to say a proper good-bye. No snoozing for the kids and me while the little fat man comes in the dark and takes you off in the kiddie car."

"Everything will be fine," Mom asserted grimly. "Nothing is going to happen.

On Tuesday morning, we'll all be together again."

"So okay. So call the little fat man and tell him not to bother comin' over here tomorrow morning," Pop said. He paid no attention to what Mom was saying.

When Pop went to take his shower, Mom looked at Jaris and Chelsea. "Your father is something else. He's making such a big deal out of this little four-day trip to New Orleans. You'd think I was in the space program being blasted off to Mars or something. You guys don't really want to get up before five tomorrow morning to ride down to the airport with me, do you? I mean, you don't usually get up until it's almost seven. You'll be bleary-eyed getting dressed. Then you have to come home and get to school. It's all so unnecessary!"

"No, Mom," Jaris insisted. "I really do want to take you to the airport in my car. It's nice when the family sees the plane off."

"Yeah," Chelsea added. "I don't even like Mr. Maynard. I bet he's a bad driver too."

Mom looked at her children and shook her head. "He has you brainwashed. It's astonishing to me how he pulls that off. You're thinking just like him now. Your father has his flaws. But I stand in awe of his ability to completely get you guys on his side—no matter," she sighed.

Jaris set his alarm for four thirty in the morning. When it rang, he couldn't believe the night had gone already. Jaris stared at the illuminated face of his clock. He thought about the day ahead, and he felt sick. Jaris hated how this was hurting Pop. It didn't matter that his concerns were foolish. He was going to be hurt. The only other time his mother had been away for more than a day was when Grandma Jessie had minor surgery. Mom stayed with her in the condo for two days. This was worse, far worse. Back then, Mom was right in town, about eight miles away, and she wasn't with Greg Maynard.

Chelsea was already up, heading for the shower.

Pop's voice rang through the house like thunder, shattering the dawn stillness.

"Off to New Orleans!" Pop bellowed. "Time for the big shot educators to swarm into that town and cause traffic jams. And I say there goes nothin'. A big waste of time. A bunch of pompous half-baked fools trying to mess up the poor kids even more."

As Pop drove Jaris's car onto the freeway, he started lecturing. "You goin' to New Orleans, Monie. Not too many years ago, they had this Katrina thing. Big hurricane! People dyin', people losin' their homes, people losin' family. I know, I know, it seems like ages ago. But those folks probably still sufferin' from it. Like men on a battlefield. You never get over it."

Pop glanced over at his wife to make sure she was listening. "So the folks you meet in the restaurants," he went on. "Or maybe the taxi jockeys, well, they ain't gonna be as efficient as you big shot teachers think they oughta be. Cut 'em some slack, babe. I know educators like Greg Maynard think they're big stuff and oughta be treated like royalty. But some of these poor devils in New Orleans, they been to hell and back."

"Good grief!" Mom moaned.

Sometimes, Jaris thought, it was hard to tell when Pop was being serious.

At the airport, Pop pulled Mom's suitcase, and Jaris carried her briefcase. Jaris glanced nervously at his father's face. Pop looked sad. He didn't look mad anymore. He just looked sad. He put his arms around Mom and gave her the longest hug Jaris had ever seen him give her. "Love you, babe," Pop whispered to her. Jaris was sure there was a catch in his voice.

"Love you back," Mom answered in a shaky voice. Both Jaris and Chelsea hugged their mother. Then she was gone in the large crowd of passengers heading through security and for the jet that would take her to New Orleans.

# CHAPTER TEN

Lydell Nelson went nervously to English class later that day. He did not expect that Mr. Myers would say anything about his journal. Lydell thought it would be weeks before the teacher found the time even to glance at it. Then he would give it a cursory look and return it to Lydell with little or no comment. Maybe he would thank Lydell for sharing the journal with him. Maybe, based on what he read, he would urge Lydell to see a counselor.

But when the class ended on that afternoon, Langston Myers said, "May I see you privately for a few moments, Lydell?" Lydell felt numb. Usually Mr. Myers referred to his students as "Mr. Spain" or

"Miss Prince." That he called Lydell by his first name surprised and frightened him a little. What was coming up? Had he been alarmed by what he read in Lydell's journal? Would he gently suggest Lydell get help?

By the time Lydell came to the teacher's desk, the class had emptied out. "Take a seat," Mr. Myers said. Lydell grew more frightened by the minute. Mr. Myers had probably decided, from reading the journal, that Lydell had serious mental problems and needed immediate therapy. Maybe he even feared that Lydell posed a threat to the other students at Tubman.

Lydell sat down. He was glad to. His legs seemed suddenly too weak to support him. He thought if he didn't sit down, he might fall down.

"Lydell," Mr. Myers asked, "the events described in your journal . . . fact or fiction?"

"They're, you know, true," Lydell answered.

"I see," Mr. Myers said. "I must tell you that your journal is very compelling. You write with power and clarity. The journal reminds me of the powerful autobiographical works of much older writers. It is quite remarkable to read material like this from a seventeen- or eighteen-year-old."

Lydell's mind was spinning. He didn't expect this. He didn't now how to react.

"You have experienced some horrifying events, Lydell," Mr. Myers continued to say, "and I salute you for coping as you have. Writing can be a great catharsis. Do you aspire to be a writer, young man?"

"I'm not sure," Lydell responded. "I'd like to go to college, but there's not much money for . . . "

"Well, we must keep in touch, Lydell," Mr. Myers advised. "I have friends in several colleges. I would be happy to assist you with scholarship opportunities. I see great raw talent in your work, Lydell. You must keep with it. You are quite good. Later on, the English department at Tubman will be announcing a contest for works of fiction. I want you to be thinking about that and to enter your work, Lydell." He handed Lydell back his journal.

"Th-thank you, Mr. Myers," Lydell gasped, clutching his journal and walking out.

Lydell saw Kevin standing over in the shadows cast by some trees near the statue of Harriet Tubman. He was watching Lydell. He had heard Mr. Myers ask him to stay after class, and he had to find out what happened.

"So, dude?" Kevin asked when Lydell drew near.

"He *liked* it, Kevin!" Lydell bubbled. "Oh man! I can't believe this. He liked it a lot. And he doesn't think I'm crazy or something. He said the English department is having a fiction contest later on and I should enter. He says he'll help me with getting scholarship money for college. Kevin, I can't believe any of this. None of it woulda happened except for you, man!"

The two boys high-fived each another and then hugged.

At the Spain house that Saturday night, Pop made spicy pepper steak. He had heard from Mom twice on Friday and already three times today. She said she was tired. And the lines to the women's restrooms were so long that they were wasting half their day waiting. Pop seemed happy about that.

"They're runnin' her ragged, and she can't even get to the potty," he said with unseemly glee.

Mom had given one presentation, and another was due tonight.

"So, you guys," Pop declared as they cleaned up the dishes, "we gotta get up early tomorrow for church."

Jaris and Chelsea looked at one another. They often went to the Holiness Awakening Church with Mom, but Pop rarely went. Sometimes Jaris didn't go either, forcing Mom to be content with just Chelsea.

"Don't look like I just invited you to be the main course at the cannibal's convention, you guys," Pop said. "The Spain family has got to be represented at church tomorrow. You want the Big Guy to forget about us Spains so that, when we call on Him, He goes, 'Who're they? I don't know 'em.' Your mom is havin' the time of her life over in New Orleans. So we gotta go there and ask Pastor Bromley to pray for the travelers and such. You know the prayer list he does."

"You're gonna ask Pastor Bromley to pray for Mom?" Chelsea asked.

"Little girl, 'course I am. You know how he prays for the sick and the downtrodden and the soldiers over there—and them that's traveling. Your mom gonna be flying home Tuesday morning. I'm not big on airplanes anyway. They got this turbulence goin' on in the plane, stuff flyin' around. Your mother could get beaned by a flying tray or something."

"There's not much turbulence between here and New Orleans," Jaris stated.

"Hey, big shot!" Pop retorted. "We don't know yet what storm is gonna pop up. The most precious lady on earth is gonna be ridin' in that plane. I want some prayers for her. I went to bed Friday night. I'm lookin' over at where she should be, and she ain't. There's an ache in my heart. Same thing gonna happen tonight and Sunday and Monday night. So you guys get ready to be prayin' and singin' at the Holiness Awakening Church tomorrow morning."

Pop turned on the TV with the remote. Then he spoke to his kids again. "Then maybe afterwards we'll stop for cheeseburgers and sodas." Pop winked.

As Jaris and Chelsea headed for their rooms, both had the same thought. Chelsea spoke first. "He really loves Mom, huh?"

Jaris nodded, "Yeah."

The next morning, Pastor Bromley seemed surprised to see Lorenzo Spain in a very nice suit. And he was ushering in his two children into one of the front pews—his tall handsome son and his pretty daughter.

"So good to see you, Lorenzo," Pastor Bromley remarked before services.

"Yeah, Pastor!" Pop replied. "Hey, when you get to the prayer list, be sure to pray for the safe return of folks traipsin' around the country on trips. Monica, she's lollygaggin' in New Orleans right now at some crazy convention. Big waste of time."

"I heard from Mattie Archer of the big honor your wife received in being chosen—" Pastor Bromley began, smiling.

"Yeah, yeah, that's all a crock, Pastor," Pop protested. "She's goin' over there to Orleans with this idiot principal of hers. He's sweet on her, you know, *bad* business. Fatso name of Maynard."

Jaris and Chelsea were cringing with embarrassment.

"I don't believe I know him," Pastor Bromley gasped.

"No surprise there," Pop declared. "He's one of those dudes never go near a church. Real sleazy character. Divorced. On the prowl for another chick. I don't think he'd mind stealin' Monica if he could."

Pastor Bromley looked horrified. He began looking around desperately for a diversion.

Jaris and Chelsea took some seats in a pew, lowering their heads.

"While you're at it, Pastor, you might say a prayer for the marriages under attack," Lorenzo Spain rattled on. "Lot of them these days. Got to keep the bonds of holy matrimony tight, eh Pastor?"

"Oh absolutely," Pastor Bromley stammered. "Ah, there's Mrs. Jenkins now. She leads the praise choir. I must get over there and talk to her about the music for today. Very nice chatting with you, Lorenzo. Yes indeed."

Pastor Bromley almost tripped over his own feet in his haste to get away from Pop.

Pop eased into the pew. "Well, that was nice," he announced. "Pastor Bromley is a good down-to-earth guy. He knows what's out there and it ain't pretty, I'm tellin' you that."

Jaris and Chelsea were both relieved when the piano and organ began to peal. A moment later, the marvelous voice of Mickey Jenkins and the others in the praise choir drowned out everything else.

That Sunday afternoon, Athena and Falisha came over to the Spain house. They planned to listen to some music Chelsea had just downloaded. Pop peered into the room and asked, "What's that weird noise, little girl?"

"Hip-hop," Chelsea answered. " It's a new group."

"Oh yeah? I wish they'd hip-hop outta here, 'cause I'm getting' a headache," Pop complained.

"Listen to this," Chelsea urged. "It's electro rock. It's got that really cool driving percussion. It's cutting edge, Pop."

Athena got up from the floor and started dancing.

"Hey, hey, hey!" Pop cried. "You gotta buy your clothes in bigger sizes. Even when you're sittin' still, they don't cover much. You don't wanna be dancin', Athena."

Falisha said, "I like the hip-hop band from Atlanta—"

"Don't play that," Chelsea cautioned.

"Why not?" Pop demanded. "Somethin' wrong with these Atlanta hip-hoppers? Lemme hear how they hip-hop in Atlanta."

Chelsea called it up on her player. She exchanged worried looks with Athena as the Atlanta band came on. It wasn't long before Pop declared, "Okay, that's enough of that. Where do you get this trash? They're goin' on about stuff little girls like you got no business thinkin' about. Shut if off. Go play outside in the sunshine. That's the trouble with you kids. You're downloading all this garbage. You should be outside listening to the birds or takin' the dog for a walk. Any of you got a dog?"

"I have a pit bull," Athena said. "But he doesn't like to be taken for a walk."

"Great. Go play with your pit bull, Athena," Pop commanded. "Go do whatever he wants, okay? Pit bulls got more sense than teenagers" He went into the living room and turned on the weather channel.

"He misses Mom so much he's been pacing around like a lost soul," Chelsea told her friends. "Mom won't be back till Tuesday. He's just gonna be like this until then."

"My parents always go on separate vacations," Athena remarked. "Mom goes to Hawaii with her girlfriends, and Dad goes to Montana to shoot animals."

Suddenly Pop yelled from the living room. "Storms whippin' up in the Gulf. They're sayin' a hurricane is sneaking around down there. It's the hurricane season, you know. She had to go to New Orleans in the hurricane season. Beautiful. That's when the airhead educators want to have their convention. In the hurricane season."

Jaris joined his father in the living room. The weather woman pointed out the location of the tropical storm. "It's pretty far from the Gulf," Jaris noted. "It probably won't go near New Orleans."

"Maybe, maybe not. Who knows?" Pop said in a suddenly agitated voice. "You can't predict these hurricanes, boy. They do what they want. They're like women. They don't listen to reason. They just go blowing around."

Sunday evening Jaris couldn't sleep. Pop was playing the radio in the room next to his the whole night, getting the latest weather reports. Jaris heard him on the phone at about ten o'clock.

"No, I don't care how the presentation went, Monie," he was telling Mom. "The whole lousy convention can take a flying leap. Y'hear? I'm thinkin' about this storm down there. Whadaya mean, it ain't nothin'? That's what they said about Katrina. And look what happened. You'd be right in the middle of it."

Pop was silent for a few moments. Mom was probably trying to reason with him. "Babe," he finally said, "can't you cut out of there right now? Weather's good now. Just let the fat man do the rest of the clap-trap and split, babe. You catch a plane for home. I'll pick you up in the morning."

There was a long silence while Mom was talking again. When Pop next spoke, his voice was hard and angry. "I don't care about all that, Monie. I don't want you flyin' out of there when the weather's bad, y'hear me? Planes go down, lady. Ain't you never heard of wind currents and stuff?"

The conversation went back and forth for a while. Finally, Pop said a reluctant good-bye and put the phone down hard. In the darkness of the bedroom, he said into the silence. "It's that freakin' little fat guy keepin' her there. He wants one more day to stroll in the moonlight with her. He ain't givin' up."

Jaris got up and gently opened the door to his parents' bedroom. "Pop, Mom'll be home Tuesday morning. I just heard the weather report. Even if the storm turns toward New Orleans, the winds won't be dangerous until Thursday afternoon at the earliest."

"Jaris, you don't know what you're talkin' about," Pop fumed. "I asked her to come home tomorrow, but she won't. Maybe she's already havin' too much fun there, y'hear what I'm sayin'? Maybe she and Maynard havin' one of those flings. That's what goes on these days on these business trips. It's a rotten, stinkin' world, boy. People no good no more. The world, it's a dark, rotten place. It's full of rats, and they eat up a man's whole world."

"Pop, it's okay," Jaris said. But his father didn't answer him.

Pop went to work as usual on Monday. Jaris and Chelsea went to school. This time, Jaris had to ignore Sereeta's suggestion not to think about tomorrow. Jaris focused on tomorrow—Tuesday, when it would all be over. Mom would be home at last.

Tuesday night, they went to the airport at seven. Mom's flight was due in at nine. Pop, Chelsea, and Jaris wandered around the airport in such an agitated state that security checked them out twice. Finally, they found the baggage claim carousel where Mom would pick up her bags.

Then they waited while Pop nervously rambled on. "Watch!" he declared. "They'll come along arm-in-arm, your mom and that little fat man. He won't let go of her a minute too soon. Who knows what went on back there—what she'll be like when—"

Jaris felt the dark thoughts flooding into his mind. Did anything happen between Mom and Mr. Maynard? Pop would be heartbroken. But that couldn't be. Mom and Pop loved each other too much. Still, Jaris couldn't help feeling anxious. In fact, for every second Mom didn't show up, he got more fretful.

"There's Mom!" Chelsea screamed.

Monica Spain came staggering toward her family. Her hair was a mess. Her clothing was wrinkled. She had a glazed look on her face. "I hate hotels," she announced, wagging her head. "I hate planes. I hate airports. I hate conventions. I can't wait to get home to my own bathroom. I hate—"

Pop broke into her monologue. He grabbed her and lifted her off her feet. He kissed her forehead, her lips, even her nose. "I love you babe," he croaked hoarsely. "I missed you."

Monica Spain's weary face broke into a grin. "Take me home," she whispered. "Just take me home, babe."

"Monie," Pop commanded, "let's get your bag and go home."

All Jaris's worries drained out of him. He had nothing to fear. He had never had anything to fear.

Mom, Pop, and Chelsea glared at the luggage passing slowly in front of them. But Jaris's thoughts were somewhere else.

"All that worrying for nothing," he was thinking. "When will I learn? I thought

Lydell was acting crazy, not talking with anybody. But he was just scared and angry over losing his dad. He was worried about how people would treat him. All he had to do was just stop worrying about what might happen. That's easy for me to say now. But it was really hard for him to do."

Jaris chuckled quietly. "I'm no better," he thought. "I've been angsting about Mom going away. Got myself good and nervous about what might happen. And nothing bad happened. In fact, things seem even better between Mom and Pop. Why do I worry so much about what *might* happen?"

Then Jaris remembered something. Sereeta and Ms. McDowell had it right. They had said it: "Don't think about tomorrow."